DOORMAN'S CREEK

Lea Schizas

CANADA

Cover Art © by TWJ Design
Layout and Book Production by Lea Schizas
eBook ISBN: 978-1-77392-096-2
Print ISBN: 978-1-77392-097-9
Visit my website: https://www.thewritingjungle.com

To my family,
who have supported my passion for writing.
Thank you.
To my readers,
my heartfelt thanks for your support.
Means the world to me.

Chapter One

Ten years ago...

"Will you just *die* already?"

With the scoop of the shovel, he struck down hard once more. The victim finally stopped moving. Placing the tool down, the aggressor's fingers flexed, releasing muscle tension. Dragging the person by the feet, he pushed the body into the waiting shallow grave in the cave, then shoveled earth back in. Satisfied and about to leave, he paused, disturbed by a sound. A moan rose from beneath the ground.

"You still alive down there?" His maniacal laugh swirled within the cavern. "Well, not for long."

He sauntered to the side, planted both feet firmly on the ground, and rolled two small boulders, one at a time, on top of the makeshift grave. Grabbing his tool and a last glance around, he strolled away with not a care in the world.

One last step remained. He obscured the cave's entrance with branches, twigs, and rocks. With a satisfied grin, he headed back to the car. He tossed the black cape in the trunk along with the two-needle knuckle brace, pulled off the latex gloves, and shoved them in a plastic bag to dispose of later.

A swift glance at his shoes, anger thread tentacles of disgust from his toes up to his spine, ending at the tips of his fingers. He snatched the winter brush and a rag on top of the spare tire and scraped the soil from underneath the soles away. Once satisfied, he shoved the rag in the plastic bag as well. Brushing off his pants, he slammed the trunk shut.

With this bothersome problem resolved, he drove away from the Creek, fulfilled, roused by the harmony of the wind and the rustling of leaves filtering through the mausoleum-like silence.

* * * *

Present Day…

Even asleep, Susan Anderson realized it was happening again. Fingers curled and clasped the bedsheet, stomach coiled, breathing quickened…

She's sitting crossed-legged by a dirt road on the outskirts of Doorman's Creek while an EMT aids her.

A car slammed against a tree emits smoke from its crushed silver hood. A police car parks nearby.

She sways back and forth while the EMT attempts to clean a gash across her forehead. Susan's attention focuses on the second EMT prepping a man on a gurney.

"What happened, madam?" asks the policeman standing in front of her.

She startles. "I…we were laughing and I…I looked out the window…" Her body quivers.

"Uh-huh, and?" The officer glances around, as though uninterested in what she has to say. He stares at his shoes and grimaces.

"He…he wasn't slowing down. I yelled for him to stop and…he…just looked at me." She stops swaying in mid-

stream and focuses on the ambulance. She shifts her body a bit to the right for a better view.

The sun's bright rays cause her to squint and glance away for a split second. Refocusing on the ambulance, an abrupt chill cloaks her. A figure stands near the ambulance door, staring right at her, dressed in black, his face veiled from the sunlight except for this supernatural grin. His head dips down a bit as though in greeting.

"Why did you want him to stop?"

She hears the officer talking, but her gaze fixates on this black-clothed silhouette of a person. She looks at the policeman for an instant, then back to the ambulance.

The entity is no longer there.

The officer nudges her shoulder…

"Susan. Susan, wake up." Richard Anderson stood over his wife and stroked her cheek. He then brushed a lock of red hair off her face.

"What?" One of her hands made its way from beneath the sheets to wipe away drool from her mouth. Sweat trickled down her nape. Fear immobilized her until the bedroom's surroundings came into focus.

Richard sat on the bed, his detective badge pinned on his belt buckle. "You were having one of those dreams again, sweetheart."

She hugged the sheet closer and inhaled deep breaths to calm her jittery nerves. "It feels so real." Nothing ever changes. The car crash, EMTs, that mysterious black-clothed entity somehow acknowledging her presence with a slight nod. It was surreal, always with that grin—light illuminated around its mouth while darkness kept the rest of the face hidden.

"Same one you've been having the past couple of months?"

Susan nodded, wiping sweat off her forehead with the edge of the bedsheet. "The same twisted nightmare. I can't figure it out. I just…I just can't seem to save you." She looked up at him for comfort. "And that Dr. Death guy…by the ambulance…"

Richard licked his lips and then smiled, lines around his blue eyes wrinkling not with age, but with that mature sexiness she loved. "Honey, please, dream of me stranded on an island with three gorgeous beauties, all of them blessed with your beautiful green eyes. No dying, okay? You'd be doing me a favor."

She pushed aside nightmare cobwebs and offered a small smile for his sake while rubbing the side of her temples. "Yeah, right. You can't handle one beauty, Mr. Lady Killer, let alone three."

Her lips twitched, that foreboding darkness threatening to swallow her emotions once again. Her female intuition was always strong, but this…she just couldn't comprehend the meaning of this nightmare torment.

Turning to one side, she stretched, curling and uncurling her toes to remove a cramp behind the right leg.

"But you have to admit, trying to tame three beauties will be fun," Richard continued, eyebrows wiggling. He ducked real quick as Susan tried to hit him over the head with a pillow.

Bending forward, he gently tilted her face up and planted a kiss on her lips. "Get up, woman, and make me some of your strong coffee I love so much. By the smell drifting in, I think Kyle's about done making breakfast."

She stared up at his ruggedly handsome face. A touch of silver recently graced his sideburns, but that only added to his sex appeal. "In your dreams."

He winked. "Might be in yours." Richard made a hasty retreat as she reached behind for the other pillow. Three long strides saw him out the bedroom door in a flash, laughing.

She remained in bed a few minutes longer, struggling to replace traces of the nightmare with thoughts of her To-Do list for the day.

No luck. Images of yellow police tape from the dream invaded her momentary tranquility.

* * * *

Kyle Anderson stood by the black marble countertop by the stove when Susan entered the kitchen. Hot sun rays threaded through the white lace curtains over the sink as he reached in the cupboard for the lime green dishes. Breakfast was done and ready to be served.

She sniffed the air. "Breakfast smells fantastic." One eyebrow arched, staring at her son. "A clean T-shirt…*and* no chains on your jeans." Susan kissed his cheek. "*You* could move into my son's room, door to your left upstairs. And stay as long as you want." A self-satisfied giggle escaped her lips.

Kyle ignored the sarcasm and continued making breakfast. He would have worn the chain if it hadn't so conveniently been misplaced. She had made it quite clear one day that he looked like one of those teenage bums hanging around the mall. It made perfect sense she would have purposely 'lost' it. No...she claimed the washer ate it.

Whatever. The same with his JERK OFF T-shirt. Mysteriously vanished.

"I don't get you. During the end of the year finals, I had to poke and nudge you to get up, and here you are fixing breakfast…*and* off for the summer."

He set the plates down. "Mom, school is…*school*." He hid his amusement behind that response, knowing it irked her referencing education as nothing special.

"School offers you an education that will eventually build your career. Don't forget that." The finger-wagging stopped.

He rolled his eyes before his usual mimicking response. "No education leads to moral decay, understood."

"Exactly." She reached for the kettle, filled it with water for some instant coffee, and placed it on the stove. Walking past him, she playfully messed up his hair.

"Mom!"

A playful grin danced on her lips. "That's for thinking I didn't realize you're teasing me about school."

Kyle's fingers raked through his hair, rearranging it to its original style; messy, pointing in every which direction. As he washed some gel off his hands in the sink, his stomach clenched. Somehow, his plans for the day were going to come out...wasn't looking forward to it.

"So, what's on your agenda today?"

Shit. "Um...I'm meeting up with Bradley and Shawn later on," he said, drying his hands with a paper towel.

Richard entered the kitchen, newspaper snugged tight under one armpit. "Well, if it isn't the all-famous Anderson chef. How's my man?"

He glanced at his dad's smile—their favorite, almost-everyday morning ritual was about to begin.

"Actually, it's Chef Extraordinaire, unless you want me to stop the breakfast bit altogether."

"No, no, no. God forbid. That'll mean your mother will start cooking." Richard feigned a shudder.

Susan giggled, swatting Richard on the shoulder. "So, go on, Kyle, what are you guys up to today?"

Richard sat at the head of the table and unfolded the newspaper.

As Linda settled in her chair, Kyle inhaled a sharp, uneasy breath, knowing how she felt about this specific place. "We're gonna go up to Doorman's Creek, hike, walk around. Maybe try to find a cave we believe we spotted last week but had no time to investigate." Without looking at her, that hallmark exhale-of-disapproval-breath of hers sounded.

"Kyle, you know how much I hate that creek and the legend that goes with it. And a *cave*?" He side-glanced, watching her head shake disapprovingly. "What's so important about this cave that you guys need to explore it?"

His brain scrambled how to answer that. It wasn't easy with that '*Mom*' concerned stare-down she was dishing out.

"Okay, if I told you some mystical force is drawing me to it, you'd worry. So I'll tell you what you wanna hear—"

"Don't be cutesy with me." She blasted him with a stern glare.

"Sorry." He paused, changing the tone of delivery. "It's not the cave as much as wanting a place to go to and chill. This is perfect. Secluded, out of the way—"

"No parents," Richard added.

"Exactly." Kyle grinned. He spotted and appreciated the twinkle and understanding in his dad's eyes.

"Well, I don't like it," Susan said. "The legend about old man Doorman still walking those paths gives me the willies." She waved her hands about in the usual manner when upset. "And what do you mean by a mystical force?"

Richard's head shook. "Geez, Susan. They're teen boys."

"Bite your toast, Richard. Anyway." She gave her husband a 'be on my side' stare before turning back to her son.

Kyle looked away; easier than facing her puppy eye pouting stares. Why couldn't she stop smothering him? *I'm fifteen already!* He finished his buttered toast and sipped his chocolate milk.

Sounding off a long, exasperated sigh, she shrugged. "I'm outnumbered, I see. Just as long as you're back by six, *the latest*, you hear?"

Kyle caught the serious tone, which meant no 'ifs' or 'buts'.

"Don't forget your grandparents are coming over tonight for a barbeque. They're leaving for their trip tomorrow."

"How long are they going for this time?" Richard asked, giving his son a thumb's up after a mouthful of his scrambled eggs, pointing to the bacon, French toast, and fruits left on his plate.

"Who knows? They're retired. If these odd trips here and there energize them, good for them."

"But, Ma, they're not normal trips. Most folks at their age go to Florida and retire there."

Susan shrugged. "So, they like to be different. Who wouldn't like to take a trip to the Andes Mountains or Tibet?"

Richard and Kyle glanced at one another. "Heck, not me!" they both answered.

"When we retire, dear husband of mine, you just may change your mind."

Richard smirked, caressing her hand. "Give me Greece, or some hot paradise like that, and I say, yes, here we come. Now that's perfect for one who has a fine eye for beauty." He pushed his plate to the side and picked up the newspaper once again, ending his part in the conversation.

Kyle prayed the discussion remained on his grandparents' trip and not Doorman's Creek. There was no way he wanted to explain that 'mystical force' comment. They never spotted a cave. Today's exploration was just a hunch from what he's been feeling the last two months about a cave. Powerful instincts pulled him toward a specific area, which ended up a bust last time, but today, they planned to head up a different path.

Several minutes later, the kitchen's back door opened.

"Yio, Mr., Mrs. A., whassup?" Sixteen-year-old Shawn Davies traipsed in as if he owned the place. Right behind this muscular teen was fifteen-year-old Bradley Dugan.

The boys leaned against the countertop.

"Shawn, Bradley, people usually knock before they walk into someone's home," Susan said, shifting her gaze from one boy to the other.

Richard looked up from his newspaper, acknowledging the boys with a slight nod. "Susan's right. I didn't hear a knock." As he returned to his reading, he added, "Next time, I just might have to arrest you boys."

Kyle was surprised to see them. "I thought we were meeting up at the creek?"

"Couldn't wait," Bradley said, nudging his head toward Shawn. "This one here had me up all night with his music."

Lowering his newspaper once again, Richard smirked. Kyle knew that nostril flared look. His dad was about to bust his muscular pal's chops.

"Shawn, why don't you try counting sheep instead of listening to your CDs to fall asleep? I hear that works."

"Yeah, right, Mr. A., like waking up with wool balls or —"

"Shawn!" Susan's nose scrunched up, obviously misconstruing what he meant.

Kyle grabbed a napkin, concealing his wide grin.

Shawn had a '*What? What did I say?*' perplexed look on his face. "No, Mrs. A., don't twist. I meant after I counted a thousand sheep, I'd have so much wool in my mouth I'd be —"

"None of your explanations, Shawn." Susan's arm extended out, palm aimed toward his face. "Just make sure Kyle's back by six. That's all! Bradley, I'm counting on you to keep an eye on these two characters."

Bradley smiled nonchalantly, his hands behind his back, feet slightly parted in a soldier's stance, nodding.

Between his two best friends, Kyle knew his mom liked Bradley the most. It was obvious from the way she spoke to Shawn she thought of him as a wannabe hoodlum waiting to grow up and cause havoc. Maybe because he loved to wear chains on his pants? Who knows? Shawn was just a muscular, handsome kid who used it to the max and tried to act all big and tough around people. He was as harmless as Mrs. Druid, their eighty-seven-year-old neighbor across the street.

Kyle stood, walked over by the door, and picked up his backpack off the floor. He had assembled a few essential items they might need in case they found the cave today.

Which he was praying they did. Another sleepless night with swirls of this cave rocketing his dreams wasn't an option.

"And, boys," Richard said as they were about to leave, "*knock* next time."

Bradley blushed and lightly punched Shawn in the arm. "Sorry."

"Sure thing, Mr. A. Hey, we're men. Don't want to step in at the wrong moment, ya' know?" Shawn gave Richard a wry smile as he glanced over at Susan.

Kyle shoved Shawn toward the back door once Bradley stepped outside. "You're gross, you know? Let's go. Bye, Ma, bye, Dad."

"Oh, no, that's fine, Kyle. I'll clean up your mess." Susan pointed to his almost empty plate still sitting on the table, tone dripping with sarcasm.

Kyle bit down on his lower lip not to snicker. "Your rules, Mom. I make breakfast, you clean up."

Shawn took this opportunity to bypass Kyle, grab a French toast from the table, then run out.

"Shawn!" Kyle closed the kitchen door behind him.

****

Carvings with 'DEATH', 'YOU WILL NEVER R.I.P.', and 'BEWARE' were visible on old, scarred trunks in Doorman's Creek as the boys trampled in-between the tall, mature trees. A flock of blackbirds cascaded above while the boys pressed onward through twigs and gnarled branches.

Kyle inhaled deeply. A blend of pine and spruce aroma tickled his senses. Peaceful. That's how he'd described this place until recently. Now the one word would be 'enigmatic'. He kicked away at the thin strewn obstructions on the ground while walking along with his friends. The disquiet of the entire place unnerved him.

"Kyle, you sure we're going the right way this time?" Shawn asked, looking all around. He bent down, removing several small twigs that found their way into his running shoes.

"It was about several yards past the dinosaur tree if my hunch is right," Kyle answered. Deep down he prayed this time around they'd find that cave because his friends, Shawn mostly, were becoming disinterested. Shawn would prefer playing soccer, movies, picking up girls...

Shawn walked over to a big, gray boulder. It cast an eerie, haunting shadow on the manmade creek, silhouetted by some tree shadings.

"I don't even remember where this dinosaur tree is." Shawn looked lost. His brows furrowed so close together that it gave the illusion of a unibrow. "And this place has no color. Bloody drab."

"Shawn, put your CD on. I think you're low on power. Kyle, you tell your parents about this feeling you got about the creek and this cave?" Bradley asked, picking up a rock, and tossing it hard across the creek. He watched it skip off the top of the water...

* * * *

Several hundred yards away, a figure carrying a woman over his shoulder moved amongst the trees. His steps were deliberate and paced, destination clear. Dusk's dim lighting didn't sway his steady movement.

The female's faint moan vibrated on his shoulder. Her chest heaved with each struggling breath.

His grip tightened around her waist.
A smile lit his face.

Chapter Two

Bradley picked up another stone and tossed it in the creek, watching it skip along the top once more.

Shawn kicked at the twigs around his feet, looking bored. Every so often, he'd reach down and pull a cluster of grass mixed with earth to shoot toward Bradley, irritating his friend.

Bradley repeated his question. "So, you tell your mom about the weird connection to this place or what? All you keep talking about is this cave. We've been coming here since before school ended and found nothing."

The squawking of birds and squirrels communicating with one another somewhere off in the distance interrupted tranquility.

Kyle shook his head. "How could I tell her anything? *I* don't understand it. I just feel drawn to this place, that's all. And that stupid cave keeps popping into my dreams like it's calling out to me. Anyway, I cracked a joke about it today, but I don't think she took me seriously."

Kyle didn't know *how* to bring up this feeling about the creek to his parents. His dad was busy with work, offering most of the time a fake smile as though listening to him. And his mom would ban him from coming here altogether if she thought it was dangerous. Which it wasn't, or at least he didn't think so. About two months ago, an impression of a cave suddenly appeared in a dream, a compulsion so great to locate it, it almost made studying for final exams a hardship. Thankfully, he passed. This surreal energy continued to push him to find the cave, but why? The only way to shake off this compulsion and pull himself together was to find it.

The massive trees stretched their branches across the sky. The dark forest blanketed the sunlight, casting shadows and cool temperatures under the boughs of the trees, obstructing the time of day it was.

"Why do we call it the dinosaur tree again?" Shawn asked, maintaining that stupefied look on his face.

Bradley shook his head at Shawn and threw another rock into the creek. It bounced three times…

* * * *

Exhausted and beyond frightened by now, she realized death was claiming her. The pain from the attack on her body dulled, but breathing became more difficult. She whimpered out several heartbreaking moans as a last resort for mercy. Her pleas went unanswered other than a laugh from her assailant.

One hand slipped to the side as the man with the black cape ambled on, oblivious and unsympathetic to her weak struggle.

Droplets of blood fell on leaves as her hand scraped against a tree's rough surface. Her body absorbed the pain but her mind did not register it.

Life was dimming.

* * * *

A squirrel jumped off a tree, startling the three boys.

"Jesus!" Shawn stumbled back a few steps.

Bradley shook with laughter. "Ooh, the Shawnster gets scared."

"Like you weren't, fuckface," Shawn hollered back, his face flame red. He bent and picked up a pebble, tossing it at Bradley's feet.

Kyle paid no attention to his squabbling friends. He walked off to the right, continuing the search for the cave, determined to find it. There was something about it grasping him, not letting go. It just kept dancing a solo in his mind, pushing all other collective thoughts away, taking the lead role.

The constant battle to decipher this powerful instinct only led to a dead-end, frustrating him. They just *had* to find it today.

A muffled sound from somewhere off in the distance caught his attention.

"Shh!" Kyle stilled and listened, motioning to his friends to be quiet.

The humming sound of bees started low until it shattered the eerie silence that enveloped Doorman's Creek.

The squirrel scurried back up the tree.

"You guys hear that?" Kyle asked, turning toward them. The hairs on the back of his neck stood at attention.

"Hear what?" Bradley upped his pace to catch up to him.

"Don't know. I thought I heard…aw, forget it. Sounded like someone moaning or something." *I must be going nuts, hearing things.*

"Ya think the Bitch Witch of the Creek is after us?" Shawn teased, biting his fingernails as though eating corn on the cob.

"You're warped, you know that?" Kyle shook his head.

"Me?" Shawn said, blowing out a heavy sigh. "What about you, and this thing you have with this godforsaken place? We've spent the better part of early warm weather on our summer vacation searching for a nonexistent cave."

Bradley walked between the two boys. "Actually, you two, there *is* a story associated with Doorman's Creek."

"*Associated?* Speak like a normal teen, man. You scare me at times." Shawn shoved Bradley gently off to the side.

Bradley scrubbed a hand over his face, composing himself, then turned to Kyle. "Like I was saying, this story that's *associated*"—He looked over to Shawn purposely, adjusting his glasses higher up his nose—"with our creek, goes back about ten years. They found two teenage girls dead, with bite marks on their necks, or at least they looked like bite marks, lying by our dinosaur tree, the one we named because it looks really old, Shawn. Remember?"

Shawn shrugged, opened his mouth to say something, but motioned Bradley to continue instead.

Kyle anxiously waited to hear the rest of the story. Anything he could find out about Doorman's Creek might help him figure out this compulsive attraction to this place. Even rumors at this point would fulfill his curiosity appetite.

"Anyway, they say the killer placed them side-by-side, facing each other," Bradley added in a 'that's about it' tone, shrugging his shoulders.

"And?" Kyle's hunger for more ate away at him. It felt like he was sitting on a jagged blade of tell-me-more agony.

"Old man Doorman, you know, the eccentric, or like we used to call him, the retard around town, was believed to have been the killer since he had a passion for vampires and such. They found no evidence against him, though. He claimed his innocence till the day he disappeared."

"What a bunch of horseshit," Shawn spat, and walked off ahead of them.

Kyle sucked in an exasperated breath of air. Why couldn't he get across to Shawn how important this was to him? Unlike Bradley, Shawn didn't believe in intuition or had any interest in Doorman's Creek. He made that perfectly clear. Just tagged along to hang out, which was fine, if he could only keep his trap shut sometimes. He watched Shawn disappear behind the big maple tree up ahead before turning to Bradley. "Did they ever find him?"

"Not that I know of. The weird part is he claimed he had a vision of who it was, but no one listened."

"Old goat," Kyle said, remembering a tale of his own with old man Doorman. "I don't know about you, but he was…from what I remember…okay. I remember him on a Halloween night, and, yeah, you're right, Brad. He did have a fascination with vampires. I remember seeing him with this black cape on, all the time, around the park. Well, we all did. Anyway, I was out with my mom one Halloween before the three of us met, he was crossing the street…and he looked at us…brought his cape to his face, and said to my mom 'I vant to suck your blood'. She laughed. The next thing we knew, someone came from behind, grabbed my Halloween bag, and took off with it. I was, what, five, six years old. Old man Doorman ran after him like a bat in hell before my mom could even react."

Bradley was practically jumping out of his clothes with excitement over this recollection. It seemed to quench his thirst to add more info to Bradley's Unsolved Mystery Scrapbook, which he really had. He loved solving puzzles. That's why Kyle blessed his lucky stars to have him as a friend right now.

"And what happened?" Bradley prodded, his glasses jiggling up and down with every head movement.

"We went home and later on that night, Doorman comes ringing our bell, handing my Halloween bag to my mom. I remember him stuttering something like 'I-I-I didn't know wh-where you-you l-lived.'"

Kyle mimicked him exactly according to Bradley's 'That's so cool, Kyle' outburst.

"And from then on, every time he'd see us, he'd wave or come over to say hi. Even as a kid, I remember people staying away from him. Mom seemed to like him. Said he was a harmless and misunderstood soul. And that's why I don't get why she's so against coming here. Or why she believes this nonsense of his ghost walking around the creek. And who the hell knows if he's dead? Everyone assumes he is, but he might have just upped and left because of everyone's stupidity against him. I mean, shit, I'd leave, too."

"Hey, guys, look over here. I think I found it," Shawn shouted not too far off.

Kyle and Bradley took off in his direction. Kyle spotted Shawn first and his breath hitched. His friend was removing branches from what appeared to be the entrance to a cave. Halting in front of their muscled friend, each boy took handfuls of broken twigs and obstructions, clearing the opening.

"Good job, Shawn," Kyle said, high-fiving him.

"Well, while you two were reminiscing about Halloween and old man Doorman, I went hunting for this mysterious cave of yours." He pointed toward it. "Found it. Thought it was a humongous boulder at first."

Bradley snickered. "Such a big word 'reminiscing'. Guess I'm a good influence on you, after all."

Shawn narrowed his eyes. "Too bad I don't have any influence on you cos you're still a skinny twerp."

Kyle stood by the opening, examining it. The entrance was just large enough for one person to enter at a time. He poked his head inside, and blinked several times, trying to adjust to the lack of light within, but no use. Kyle stood back again.

"Can't see a thing in there it's so dark. Shawn, get me my backpack. I dropped it over there." He pointed to its location.

A few seconds later, he rummaged through his bag, took out his flashlight, and disappeared inside.

"You know, a bear might be in there," Bradley warned, hesitating at the entrance.

"Then we better make sure Smokey doesn't catch and fine us for littering his forest," Shawn joked, pulling Bradley into the cave with him, right behind Kyle.

"I've got a bad feeling about this," Bradley said, then jerked free from Shawn's grip on his T-shirt.

"Will you guys stop arguing?" Kyle shouted from inside just as the two boys entered the cave.

The cavern opened up the further in they walked. A big enough hole at the top allowed some light to flicker through, amplifying the flashlight's illumination. There was a dank odor emanating from the air; various-sized worms, moist soil, and rocks covered the ground. There only appeared to be one opening, the one they came through, no endless tunnels like a maze.

"This is so…" Shawn began.

"Dark!" Bradley finished.

"Exactly. Dark and scary. Soon…we shall be in the tomb of…Dracula." Shawn drawled out a heavy Count accent, his arm to his mouth as though covering it with a cape.

"Hope he bites your ass," Bradley muttered.

With two fingers, Shawn made the sign of the cross toward his friend.

"Come on, you two," Kyle snapped. "Let's move up a bit."

"Yeah, Bradley, listen to our brave leader."

"Geez," Kyle grunted, letting out an exasperated sigh.

"What? I'm serious!" Shawn defended. "You're always thinking."

"Thank God someone is," Bradley added, smirking.

Before Kyle had a chance to tell them to stop fooling around, Shawn rushed up, pinned Bradley's head under his right armpit, then maneuvered a wrestling pull-down. They playfully fought on the ground, scattering the cave's soil about.

Kyle watched them act like kids and couldn't help smiling. They were who they were and no way would he change them. That's what made their friendship so special.

"Hey, guys, watch out for those boulders." The boys scrimmaged too close to what Kyle perceived as a possible danger to themselves.

As he made a step to separate them, something protruding from the earth right beside Shawn caught his attention.

Shawn stopped and stared at it, too. "Hey, look here. Our first discovery as archaeologists," Shawn said, clearing the soil around this faded white object with his hands.

Kyle moved in closer to get a better look while Bradley dusted himself off.

* * * *

The man halted, then dropped the woman with red polished nails like a sack of rocks by a tree somewhere in Doorman's Creek. She let out an awful, gurgling sound before exhaling her last breath.

He stared for several minutes at her blank hazel eyes gaping back at him, the once sparkling life now extinct. A sense of gratification hit, not emotional, but at another accomplishment. He kicked a few sporadic leaves on top of her, brushed the dirt off his shoes, then walked away calmly.

* * * *

Shawn jumped back, eyes wide, staring at the object. "Oh shit, what the…"

Kyle approached and swept away more earth around it to get a better look.

All three stared at one another, startled to see they had just uncovered part of a skeleton. Unsure of their next move, they simply ogled it for several minutes, fascinated.

"Is it human, Bradley?" Kyle finally asked. Amongst the three, Bradley was the most interested in forensics and anything to do with mysteries. And Kyle was hoping Bradley would confirm what he already suspected from the little they could see.

Bradley crouched beside the partially exposed skeleton, inspecting it. "Not an expert, but it sure looks like a human skull."

Chapter Three

Susan and Richard stood in their backyard with her parents. The sweet scent of the hanging petunia and carnation baskets mingled with the rose bushes around the trellised patio filled the air. But their relaxing aroma was not enough to get that insurmountable worried feeling out of Susan.

"Now, dear, boys will be boys. You know, he probably lost track of time with his friends," said her mother, giving Susan a gentle hug.

"Stop defending him, Ma. I warned him to be here on time to see you both before leaving for your trip." Susan shrugged off her mom's sympathetic touch and immediately regretted it. The genuine smile on her mother's lips slackened into a frown, the happiness in her eyes gone.

"I'm sorry. I'm…I'm just upset. I didn't mean to snap at you." She took a hold of her mom's hand and patted it. Susan let out a soft sigh, noticing the compassionate smile back on her lips.

Her father slowly rose from the lawn chair and approached his daughter. "Let him be, already. The boy is getting older. He needs some freedom." His arthritic, swollen hands quivered as he shook them to make a point.

"It's about responsibility, Pops," Richard said, turning over the steaks on the barbeque. "He's an hour late. Besides, we had a recent disappearance…" Richard cut his sentence short and quickly glanced at Susan.

She sucked in a deep breath, warding off a bad feeling.

Tugging on his T-shirt, Susan motioned for him to follow, away from her parents.

Richard handed the tongs to his father-in-law, slapping him on the shoulder. "I'll be right back. Don't burn the steaks now," he jested.

The old man looked at him and amplified a big 'humph'.

After walking a short distance from her parents, Susan whispered, "I'm worried. He's always called when he's late." She looked up at the night sky housing a thick bank of dark gray clouds. The humidity in the air and the bleak showing of the clouds indicated a rainstorm. Susan exhaled heavily, turning her focus to Richard once more.

"Okay, honey, let me call Bradley's house. No use calling Shawn's. His mother probably doesn't know what time of day it is, anyway." They both knew Shawn's mom hit the bottle often. It's a surprise Shawn grew up to be such a good kid, considering the lack of supervision or house rules surrounding him. Although Susan still held some reservations about Shawn's friendship with Kyle.

Removing his cell phone from his pocket, he started to dial Bradley's house when Kyle walked through the opened gate. Susan took in his attire–torn and dirty.

"Where the hell have you been?" Richard spat, unable to control his temper in front of the in-laws.

Susan was appalled as she stared at Kyle's disheveled clothes. Dirt smudged his face, down his neck, and his fingernails were covered with traces of soil. His backpack displayed the same wear and tear. "Look at you! You look as if you were excavating."

Gazing at the ground, Kyle sidestepped around his parents. "How's it going, grandma, gramps?" He kissed both of them.

His granddad leaned toward him and whispered, "You're in hot poo with your mom, son."

"I heard that, Dad. Go inside, Kyle, and wash up. We'll discuss this later," Susan said. Her hand froze in mid-air, stopping whatever Kyle was about to say. "Please, go wash up."

Kyle noticed that angry nostril-flaring she does when upset. This gave him a pretty good indication of how much trouble he was in. *Grounded for sure.*

Richard wrapped an arm around his son's shoulders and directed him toward the kitchen. Kyle's nerves rattled as the mounting grip around his shoulders tightened. He gave a glance at his dad and spotted the famous Richard 'ugly-neck-gland twitching, get-out-of-my-way' look. *Yep, I'm dead.*

Once inside and the back door slammed shut, Kyle placed his backpack on the table. He walked to the opposite end from where his dad stood.

"Kyle, you scared the shit out of us tonight."

Yep, I'm in trouble, big time. One thing his father never did, and that was to swear in front of him. Unless he was really and truly angry. Although shit wasn't really a swear word, technically. Then again, according to his mom, it was whenever *he* said it.

"Sorry, Dad, but we were exploring the cave and by the time we knew it, it was…night." Kyle hoped the apologetic tone used would ease his dad's nerves a bit. He stared at his face, the few wrinkles more defined with each infuriating grimace.

Richard straightened his shoulders. "Kyle, listen to me…and get that dirty sack off the table!"

Without hesitation, Kyle reached over and shouldered his backpack. Afterward, he kept his head down, avoiding eye contact.

Richard cleared his throat. "In my line of business, I know what can happen and how easy it is for a child to go missing."

Kyle shook his head, looking up. "That's the problem, Dad. You and Mom keep referring to me as the child. I'm responsible!" Kyle's earlier objective was to take whatever his father was going to dish out, but once that word 'child' crept up, ire erupted.

"Well, prove it to me, for crying out loud! Don't show up whenever you feel like it. I'm pretty sure the young lady that went missing said the same thing to her parents." Richard's veins on the side of his neck popped up a storm.

Kyle stood back for a second and let his father have his say. There was no use arguing and defending himself because he *was* guilty. Lost track of time. The biggest question occupying his thoughts now was whether this was the right time to tell him about their find.

"Anyway, you can forget about the cave tomorrow if you had any intentions of going back."

Kyle's jaw dropped. "Dad! We have—"

Richard looked at him sternly. "We're taking your grandparents to the airport. That's it! Now go upstairs and wash up."

Kyle shoved his backpack in front of him and gave it a light punch before turning to leave without another word. Heading up the staircase to his bedroom, he heard the kitchen door open, then slam shut.

Tossing the backpack by the side of his bed, he ambled toward the window.

The prior black ominous clouds threatening rain had dispersed. A crescent moon decorated the almost cloudless night. There was always something about the night sky that calmed him down, and tonight was no exception.

After several minutes, Kyle looked down spotting his neighbor, twenty-something or other Lewis McGuire kissing a nice-looking brunette in jeans, right outside his driveway. The moon's beam gave Kyle just enough light, along with the flickering streetlight on the edge of his front lawn, to see her pretty smile as she wrapped her arms around Lewis' neck. Feeling like a Peeping Tom, he stepped back, closing the blinds.

* * * *

Kyle crouched down, tying his running shoes by the main entrance. He could feel his mom staring at him.

"Remember, behave!" she said.

Kyle drew in a deep breath. Throughout the ride back home from the airport, that's all she kept saying. It took all of his calm energy to convince her to go to Bradley's for the night. "Yes, and I'm sorry about yesterday, Mom. I didn't mean to worry you." There was a pang of regret for what he put his parents through last night. It never crossed his mind she'd think he might have been the next missing person blasting all over the local news.

Getting up, he spotted her outreached hand aiming for his hair and ducked just in time.

"I love you, sweetie," Susan said, almost in a whisper.

His gaze swept over her. "Mom, I'm just sleeping over at Bradley's." Kyle put on his baseball cap.

Richard came down the stairs in his shorts and T-shirt at that moment. "Your mother dreamed of you, instead of me, in trouble, so she's worried."

"You're having weird dreams?" This surprised him. An urgency to clue her in for a split second on his intuitions lately about Doorman's Creek hit him but decided against it at the last second. It would be a stupid move that would have him house-jailed for the entire summer under her watchful eye. *Yeah, no way.*

"It's nothing," she said, closing her eyes, and repeating, "It's nothing" while shaking her head gently.

Kyle heard the worried tone, impeccably polished by her stance. The way she avoided looking at him, her twitching lips; these were signs Kyle had come to know when she was at odds with a problem.

"No, seriously, Mom. Maybe I can help you. I got so much info on dream interpretations when I did my English project last year."

Susan looked at him intensely, obviously intrigued. "Like what?"

"Susan, leave him alone. You two can interpret your dreams tomorrow," Richard said in a brusque tone. He wrapped his arm around her shoulder, sliding her a step back from Kyle and the front entrance.

"Kyle, just be careful. That's all. Don't do anything foolish with your friends today. And make sure you call us tonight. We'll be at Karen's house. You remember the number?"

"Implanted in my head." He debated whether to pursue the dream conversation, but the way his dad interjected earlier gave him the sign to simply drop the subject. He'll approach her another time when they're alone.

After opening the door, Kyle turned, hugged her, and saluted his father like a soldier, then left.

Susan closed the door and faced Richard. "You're no help, you know?" she spat, shaking his arm off her shoulder.

"I was just trying to get him out the door so we can be alone, Mrs. Anderson. All morning, seeing people kissing at the airport got me in a horny mood."

He offered a mischievous grin before pulling her closer, kissing her neck, and slowly pushing down the straps of her tank top.

"I'm worried about him," she mumbled.

"He's a big boy. Concentrate on *this* big boy right now. I need these clothes *off*," he growled. He continued caressing her body, nibbling on her ear.

She inhaled a few calming breaths. "I'm serious, Richard. I have these godawful bad vibes." She tried to loosen his hold on her but to no avail.

"I talked with him last night. He won't pull another stunt like that again, okay? Now, can we move on to a more sensual note?" A long, exasperated breath touched her neck.

He gently placed his hands on her face, kissing her pouting lips. "I wanted you all morning."

"What, right here, in the middle of the hallway?" She tilted her head to the side, and his sly grin reappeared, melting her instantly.

"Hey, we've tried everywhere else." He wiggled his brows, offering a boyish smirk.

Susan laughed and shrugged him off. "I'll race you upstairs. The first one up the stairs gets to play the rider."

Richard sidestepped past her, took one long step, and sprinted up the stairs. "Guess I'll be the rider." He turned to her, grinning from the top landing.

"Just the way I like it." She looked up, forcing a smile.

She gave one long stare at the main door, trying to shake off this impending doom gripping her insides before walking upstairs.

"Oh, Kyle…I hope you guys stay out of trouble," she whispered, making sure Richard didn't hear.

Chapter Four

Kyle walked down his driveway toward the sidewalk when he heard Lewis McGuire call out his name from next door. He stopped and waited in silence for the denim-decked neighbor to approach.

"Hey, puke, caught you staring last night," Lewis said, his six-foot frame towering over Kyle in a menacing stance, glaring down at him.

"What are you talking about?" Kyle took a step back to add more room between him and the red-faced neighbor. His cheeks blazed with embarrassment over his little staring fiasco last night. Didn't think Lewis had seen him.

"You seemed pretty interested in my girl last night. Or were you studying my kissing moves?" Lewis' eyebrows raised, a wide grin forming.

As if, you moron! "No way." *What an egotistical asshole.* "I just happened to look outside, and there you were, in front of *my* lawn, making out."

"Just teasin', relax." Lewis set off a stream of curt, bark-like laughter. "She's a looker, though. Her name's Frances. Met her last night, at a club."

"That's nice. She have a sister?"

"What, for you? Get lost!" Lewis shoved Kyle's head to the side and walked off.

"Nice talking to you too… *asshole*," Kyle muttered as he took off for Bradley's house.

* * * *

Bradley shuffled through some papers on his desk cluttered with years of accumulative newspaper clippings, relics of past unsolved cases. His mahogany desk matched the somber tan walls plastered with more clippings but framed to add some 'class'. Anyone walking in would think they just stepped into an investigative task room.

Shawn lazily sprawled on Bradley's bed, eyeing Kyle talking on the phone. He sank his teeth into the last bit of his bagel and tossed the napkin in Bradley's trashcan.

"We're going to head up to the park soon, play some soccer. I'll call you back tomorrow morning, Mom," Kyle lied, giving that '*What do you want me to do?*' stare at his friends, slightly embarrassed having to give his every move to his mom in front of his pals.

"Don't be too late, *please*, sweetie."

"We won't be late, Ma. I promise. See you tomorrow. Bye." Kyle hung up and walked up to Bradley. He gave Shawn a stern look after an unsuccessfully suppressed giggle escaped his friend's lips. "So, did you find the article?"

"No, but I know it's here somewhere," Bradley said, picking up and inspecting more papers.

Shawn, apparently flustered watching Bradley thumb slowly through the stack of so-called clutter, trotted over to the desk. "How can you find anything here?" He started tossing papers off the desk.

"Stop!" Bradley grasped his arm and swung it away. "It's an *organized* mess, okay? I have everything exactly where I want it." He picked up an old newspaper clipping and shoved it in Shawn's face. "*Here*… here it is."

"Touchy much?"

"You don't understand. This"–Bradley pointed around to his room–"might seem like a disorganized mess to you, but it's meticulously set up in an order I want, the way I like it, got it?"

"Like I said...speak like a normal teen, will ya?" Shawn raised his hands in surrender mode. "I get it. Chill, okay? I was just trying to help."

Kyle rubbed his temples. "Oh, my God! You guys are giving me a migraine. Can we just, for one night, team up with no arguments? And, Shawn, you sleep here at least three times a week—you never once picked up Bradley's *touch-and-your-dead* attitude when it comes to his hobby? Seriously?"

"Honestly, I crash in the TV room downstairs or a sleeping bag on the floor here after we've played games all night."

"After *you* play games all night," Bradley corrected.

Shawn was about to say something when Kyle stuck his hand up. "Drop it. Let's just see what the article says."

With no other outburst, the three of them sat on the bed as Bradley started to read from the clipping.

"Saturday, July 16, 1992. Two more teens go missing. Barbara Cambridge, 16, and Delilah Coolidge, 17, were last seen leaving a party in the suburban district of Hampstead approximately 12:30 a.m. Anyone with any information, please contact Sergeant McGuire at—"

"Hey, isn't that your neighbor, Kyle?" Shawn asked.

Kyle nodded but kept his focus on Bradley. "Where's the one where they find them?"

Bradley got up, walked to his desk, and opened a drawer. Rummaging for a couple of seconds, he finally retrieved a scrapbook.

"You say *I'm* warped? You've got a scrapbook filled with articles on dead people, for crying out loud," Shawn jeered.

"Unsolved crimes. Not dead people," Bradley corrected.

"What's the dif?"

"Forget it." Bradley shook his head, giving up explaining to his friend, who had a look of '*What?*' plastered on his face.

"No, I wanna hear this." Shawn wasn't giving up. He crossed his arms across his chest, glaring and waiting for a response.

Bradley heaved a long sigh, shifting his weight from one foot to the other. "It's not hard, Shawn. An unsolved crime is exactly what it means. I like to figure out unsolved crimes, cold cases or not. It's my interest. I'd like to be a detective one day. And these disappearances are intriguing to me. They're like puzzles to put together."

Kyle swore softly under his breath. "Show me the article." An edge of frustration marked his tone as he bypassed Shawn to stand beside Bradley.

Opening the scrapbook to the article, Bradley handed it to Kyle, who started to read out loud. "Tues. Apr 21, 1993, the bodies of teenagers Jennifer Welt and Sarah Bondman, both 17, were discovered early this morning by a passer-by, out jogging in the early hours of the day."

Kyle closed the scrapbook and looked up at his friends, his heart pounding fiercely in his chest. "It's *not* the same girls from the first article! You were right, Bradley!" Kyle couldn't contain his enthusiasm. He got up and paced back and forth.

"What are we gonna do?" Shawn asked, staring at Kyle as he made a path from the desk to the bed and back again.

Kyle stopped and stared at his buddies. Bradley's clock on the wall ticked away loudly, as though just as excited by this new development.

Tick…Tick…Tick…

Kyle's mind absorbed the revelation, stored it, and exploded with excitement.

"We're going back to the cave to see if there's another body. If Bradley's right, and it's the same killer, then it makes sense he would have buried the other girl close by."

"And then?" Shawn asked. Both buddies gazed at Kyle with wide-eyed enthusiasm.

"We become famous," Kyle said, high-fiving his friends.

Chapter Five

The moon's illuminating rays gleamed above the trees. The hooting of the owls, distinct in the quiet night, greeted the boys. Fallen branches crunched beneath their feet as they marched toward the cave. A few exposed gnarled stumps were so high the boys, at times, had to be careful not to trip over them.

"I hope your mom doesn't call, Kyle. Then we're all in big shit for sneaking out in the middle of the night," Bradley said.

"As if she'd call at one in the morning, you moron. And what about your mom? You don't think we'll get into big shit if she discovers we're missing?" Shawn said, whopping Bradley over the head playfully.

"Quiet! You guys are impossible," Kyle said. As different as they were in size and looks, they both had one thing in common: they struggled not to act like buffoons most of the time.

"Who we gonna disturb?" Shawn said, pointing toward the trees. "The owls? Hell, they're up and having a party. Listen to them."

They continued walking until they reached the cave entrance. Kyle stood for a bit, staring at it. A feeling of desperation snagged his senses suddenly. Something was here, something drawing him to this cave more than the mystery of the missing girls from the cold case, and he aimed to find out what it was. He opened his backpack and took out three flashlights and three small spades.

"Here, grab one." Kyle handed one to each of them. "Took them from the shed. My dad always buys more when something's on special. Drives my mom nuts."

Shawn lit the flashlight under his chin and made a spooky face. "I'm scared. Drip, drip." He motioned to his nose as if infested with nose drippings. "Demons are all around us."

Bradley swiped him across the shoulder, knocking Shawn's flashlight to the ground. It bounced off a big rock before rolling down a slope into bushes.

"Nice going, asshole," Shawn said. "Must have knocked the batteries out. How the hell are we going to find it now?"

"Come on, guys. I feel like a referee all the time." Kyle tried to diffuse the tension between them, as always. "Shawn, stay in the middle of us so you don't get lost."

"As if…" Shawn kicked small rocks toward Bradley.

Without another word, the boys entered the cave, aiming the two flashlight beams ahead against the perpetual darkness. A rat jumped out of nowhere, startling them. Shawn tried to kick it out of the way, missed and stubbed his foot against a boulder. The rat whipped by them.

"Fuckin' thing was huge," Shawn exclaimed. "Did you guys see it?" He leaned against the cave wall, took off his shoe, and rubbed his toe for a few seconds.

"Does every sentence have to be 'fucking this' or 'fuck that'?" Bradley said, shaking his head.

"Fuckin' right." Shawn grinned and put his shoe back on.

Kyle continued to the spot where they first discovered the skeleton, ignoring them. "Okay, here's the victim, skeleton, whatever…"

Bradley walked up to him, inspecting the area around the partially revealed skeleton. "I think we should start digging here, sort of like in a triangle. I'll start at the top part, Kyle, you to the right, and Shawn, you go left."

They positioned themselves in a triangular shape and were about to dig when Kyle stopped and looked back at his backpack.

"Hold on. I forgot to take out my tape recorder." Kyle rushed to his bag.

"You brought a tape recorder?" Shawn asked.

"If we're going to be famous, we might as well have our evidence recorded," Kyle said, catching the wide grins of 'Oh Yeah!' on his friends' faces.

"See, I told you. Leader," Shawn said, patting Kyle on the back.

"You know, we could easily have recorded on our phones–" Bradley began, reaching into his back pocket.

"Yeah," Shawn said, "but the problem with that is, one, I don't have a phone cos I can't afford it. And two–"

"No two," Kyle said. "I don't trust phones to not go wacky in a tech glitch, that's all."

Bradley removed his hand from his back pocket. "Shit. Either I left my phone on my desk or it dropped out of my pocket somewhere."

"Sorry, man. Hope it wasn't expensive cos your mom's gonna kill you," Shawn said.

"And that's precisely why I prefer old-fashioned tape recorders. I've already broken one phone and lost another." Taking out a tape from his jean pocket, Kyle placed it in the tape recorder. "Okay, Bradley, I'll start it off and you repeat what you said about the killer."

"What do you want me to do?" Shawn asked.

"Be the boner, you know, yourself." Bradley snort-giggled.

"Ha, ha! Funny guy." Shawn made an obscene gesture with his hand near his crotch.

"Here we go," Kyle said, placing the recorder on a nearby boulder. He clicked it on and motioned for them to be quiet. "I, Kyle Anderson, Bradley Dugan, and Shawn Davies are inside a cave at Doorman's Creek where we've discovered a human skeleton." Kyle motioned for Bradley to take over the recording of events.

"We're assuming it's the body of either Barbara Cambridge or Delilah Coolidge, gone missing in July, nineteen…nineteen…"

"Nineteen ninety-two. See, I pay attention," Shawn stated.

Drawing in a deep breath, Kyle trotted over to the recorder and turned it off. "Only info, Shawn, no extras."

Shawn shrugged his shoulders. "*Whatever*."

Kyle turned the recorder on, walked back a short distance to his spot, and signaled Bradley to continue.

Bradley ogled Shawn as he started talking once again.

"We're going to start digging to find the other body since we believe it's the same killer as Jennifer Welt and Sarah Bondman, it would make sense he would have buried them side-by-side, similar MO as with Barbara Cambridge and Delilah Coolidge."

Kyle mulled over whether to shut the recorder once they start their digging, but decided against it. He figured the more evidence they collected on tape, the more believable their story will be to whoever listens to it. And hearing them digging was evidence.

He peered over his shoulder several times. An eerie feeling of being watched came over him. His stomach twisted into knots, his heart thumped a heavier beat, and, for a mere second, an urge to run out of the cave crossed his mind. He looked toward his friends, but they seemed oblivious to anything strange…other than the skeleton. He kept this creeping sensation to himself and started excavating along with his friends.

Intense in their digging, the boys were startled when the tape clicked off out of the blue.

Kyle walked over and picked it up, inspecting it. "Did you guys touch the tape?"

Shawn stood there, brows furrowed, looking confused. "What?"

"Did you guys fool around with the tape?" Kyle asked again, agitated.

"When?" Shawn asked. "We were digging right along with you. Unless you went blind, then no."

Shawn and Bradley exchanged glances at one another before turning their focus back on Kyle.

"Forget it. Let me rewind it."

Kyle played back the tape to the point they had left off, listening to his recorded voice. "'We're going to start digging to try and find…'" He stopped the tape and glanced about. That feeling of being watched crept inside him again. Stronger. A frosty breeze, like being touched from beyond the grave, passed through him. "Did you guys feel that draft?"

Shawn and Bradley looked at each other again, a questioning leer on both of their faces.

"What are you talking about? What draft?" Bradley asked.

Shawn pointed all around. "Unless there's a backdoor, where would the draft come from?"

"You know what," Kyle began, anxiety kicking into high gear, "it's weird, but I feel like there's someone here with us." He couldn't shake this premonition, chest constricted with unease.

Shawn stared down and pointed to the skeleton. "There is." And laughed.

Kyle half-heartedly chuckled but glanced about one more time before restarting the tape. "No, it was something else. Anyway, forget it." He pressed the record button.

About to step back to his position to dig, Kyle suddenly felt like his mouth had just got stuffed with a handful of cotton balls. He started to shake as if going into an epileptic seizure. His eyes opened wide, pupils moving left and right like he was reading a cue card. He felt his heart quicken just as a chilling sensation drifted inside his body.

Shawn and Bradley immediately tossed their shovels to the ground and rushed to him, shouting, "Kyle! Kyle!" in the same panicky, high-pitched tone.

As the boys approached, Kyle drew his arms back and then pushed outward with such force they went flying, slamming against the far cave wall, about four feet away. They tumbled to the ground, unhurt but shaken, looking up at their friend in disbelief.

Kyle struggled to get his bearings, to focus on them. His focal point blurred and then cleared when a vision of a girl, in her late teens, dressed in blue jeans and a white t-shirt. She kept looking back as she ran away from something…or someone, a frightened expression on her face. Kyle distinctly heard footsteps, hers and someone else's, chasing her.

She stopped at one point, turned, and screamed, "Please, leave me alone. I don't want to die! Please!! No!!"

A nauseating chokehold gripped him when that vision changed. The girl was now sprawled by a large tree in the forest, beside another female, both of them dead by the way they slumped against one another; two distinctive marks on their necks visible to him from the angle of their tilted heads.

The vision came to an abrupt end. That same chill as before rushed down his spine before whipping out of him. Kyle stood for a split second, staring blankly ahead. He tried to move but collapsed to the ground, hitting the side of his head against one of the two boulders nearby.

He could hear Bradley and Shawn yelling, asking if he was okay, but his body was numb, paralyzed. It felt like his brain was seeping out of his skull. Pain overwhelmed him. Every sound amplified, blasting through his ears. Kyle felt as though in a dream, alive but non-functional. The surroundings grew darker. Just before he lost consciousness, his last vision was a shimmering glow right over the skeleton.

"Oh shit, shit! What the hell are we going to do, Shawn?" Bradley yelled frantically.

"What the hell was that?" Shawn stood over Kyle, flabbergasted. He crouched down to check on his friend.

"Okay, he's still breathing. Grab the recorder and help me pick him up."

Bradley, in a state of shock, kept staring down at Kyle.

"Bradley, help me pick him up, *now*!"

Shawn's anxious tone snapped Bradley out of his stupor. He grabbed the tape recorder, shoving it into Kyle's bag at the last moment.

They lifted their friend off the ground and headed for the exit.

Chapter Six

Richard sat by Kyle's hospital bed while Susan paced the floor. Kyle was eager to tell them about his adventure. The more he talked, the less his mother would have a chance to put in a word and blast him. He was hoping the hospital surroundings might encourage her to have some sympathy for him. However, by her stiff expression, tightly clenched fists, and heavy nostril-flaring exhales, this plan remained sketchy.

"It's weird, although I never went into Doorman's Creek…well…farther in than normal, I knew we were on the right path until Shawn discovered the cave. And… I don't know how to explain it, but… I had this feeling I was being guided. But I wasn't scared. It's the weirdest thing, dad."

Susan stopped pacing, ground her teeth, and glared at him.

Kyle steeled himself.

"What, in God's name, possessed you kids to go there, in the middle of the night, no less!" As expected, her tone was shaky, eyes a raging storm of emotion. His mom was a tough lady. Rarely did she ever cry, but she was close to that stage now.

Silence greeted her outburst.

Kyle eyed his dad, pleading for some support right now. A glimmer of hope emerged when his dad turned to stare at his wife.

Richard toward the door. "Honey, why don't you go to the cafeteria and get us some coffee, okay?"

Kyle exhaled a heavy but thankful sigh.

About to leave, Susan turned and gawked at him. "By the way, in case you're wondering," she said, "we drove your friends home. And let me tell you, it'll be quite some time before you're all allowed a sleepover, my friend." With that, Susan left, shutting the door behind her, but not before Kyle heard her muttering, "I can't believe this!"

Richard approached his son. "What the hell am I going to do with you? It's bad enough your mom wakes me up at night with her Dr. Death character. Now I have to worry about your premonitions too?"

Kyle couldn't believe what he was hearing. He knew his mom was having dreams, but not specifically about one character haunting her. This intrigued him.

"Dad, listen, I'm not joking. I felt like someone was guiding me, trying to show me something." He had to make his father believe him. He just *had* to.

"You had a mild concussion, probably dreaming."

Kyle shook his head, frustrated. What else could he say to convince him? "Dad, will you listen to me? I was awake and aware of everything going on. Shawn and Bradley were scared out of their wits, but I was in some sort of trance, frozen, couldn't move or talk to them but sensed them still with me."

"Okay, let's start from the beginning. You guys found this skeleton, which, for God's sake…" Richard shook his head. "…you know better than to tamper with evidence. You should have told me right away." His dad's mood, by all means, wasn't jubilant. Pure, angry energy and flaying arms erupted.

"I'm sorry. But you know my fascination with strange phenomena, and, boy, did we hit the jackpot. Besides, Dad, we didn't touch or disturb anything. We simply brushed around it." He paused, hoping this would calm his dad down a bit. But by the continued plastered and very animated frown, Kyle didn't think the muse worked.

"What about this vision?" Richard ran a hand through his hair.

"Back up, Dad, you don't want to hear about me being possessed?"

"Kyle, don't be silly."

"Thanks...forget it... Just go out there and sign my admission papers for the loony bin, then." Kyle figured if his dad didn't believe him being possessed, then the vision wouldn't be believable either. He stared long and hard at him, pouting, hoping to wear his father down to actually listen to him instead of standing there and making him feel as if he'd just committed a crime. Well, maybe they had by not revealing their find.

Closing his eyes for a split second, then exhaling deeply, Richard said, "I'm sorry, Kyle. Go on."

BINGO!

Kyle allowed a smile to curve his lips and tried to sit up. The room spun, and yesterday's lunch–the last meal he remembered eating–threatened to spill all over the hospital bed.

"Whoa, sport, stay put." Richard propped Kyle's pillow in a more comfortable sitting position.

Kyle shoved his father's helping hands aside. His determination to detail his encounter outweighed the compulsion to toss his guts. Ignoring the stomach cramps pinching his insides, he turned to his father. "Dad, listen to me. I felt like I was being guided to the cave. So, we find this thing, that skeleton head, and I kept getting this feeling like we were being watched."

"And there was no one else in there with you guys?"

Kyle shook his head as Richard stood up and walked to the bottom of the bed. Excitement elevated, knowing he had his father's interest right now.

"You sure there was no one else lurking somewhere?" Richard repeated, persistent in this grounded question.

"Positive. The next thing I knew, I felt this…this energy come into me and I got a vision of a girl running. She was scared, Dad. I could feel her fear. And someone was chasing her."

"You see him?" Richard leaned forward, gripping the metal bars of the side rail of the bed while his gaze focused on Kyle.

"No, but I knew there was someone there because she kept yelling at him to leave her alone, looking over her shoulder several times." Kyle felt dizzy once more but suppressed the need to lie back down.

"Okay, sport. Let's continue this later. You look like you could use some rest."

"No! I have to tell you *now*. My vision changed and the next thing I know, I see two girls…*dead*…by the dinosaur tree."

Richard had a confused look on his face. "Two girls now…dinosaur tree?" He turned his back and started to walk toward the door.

"Where are you going?" He couldn't believe his dad would walk out at this point.

"Just checking to see if your mom's coming. I don't want her to hear any of this, especially about seeing dead girls. That Dr. Death character from her dreams has her already spooked."

Kyle didn't hesitate a minute seeing his father's continued interest. "The dinosaur tree is this huge tree, really old, in the Creek. Anyway, the thing about the girls I noticed were these bite marks on their necks."

Kyle spotted the change in demeanor by the way his dad's shoulders pulled back as he turned around. That look of nonbeliever was now stripped and replaced with a curious stare. Richard had stopped walking and glared at his son.

"Bite marks? You sure?"

"I saw them, plain as day, Dad."

It took one long stride to stand beside his son's bed. Richard's face went pallid, and he glared at Kyle. "This is *very* important. Are you sure you saw bite marks and not scratches…or dirt…or…or something like that?"

"Dad, there were two bite marks on each of the girls' necks, and they were topless."

Richard took a step back, his hands clasped on top of his head. "Oh. My. God. There's no way you could have known this."

"What?" Kyle asked, startled by the unexpected outburst, yet excited at the same time. Something he said finally turned his dad into a believer.

"These bits of information you're telling me, we kept it under wraps so we wouldn't get copycat murders." Richard did a 360 before facing Kyle again, lowering his hands from the top of his head.

"You believe me now?" Kyle sat back against his pillow to let the nauseating feeling leave him. But his adrenaline was pumping hard now.

"Kyle, I don't want you to mention this to anyone, *especially* to your mother, you hear?"

As if. The last thing he wanted was to worry his mom. She'd have him under house arrest for the rest of his life. "Dad, there's something else." Kyle tensed, hesitant to reveal his next intuition. He shuddered, trying to figure out how to word this next revelation.

"What?"

"I don't know how to explain this; it's just…just a feeling I kept getting."

"What, Kyle?"

Painstakingly, he took the open invitation to continue. "When I was possessed…in this trance or whatever it was, I kept getting this feeling, or I was made to feel something about…about a cop?"

"A cop? What do you mean?" Richard furrowed his brows, an ice-cold stare at the mention of 'cop'.

"I don't know, Dad. That's the only thing I'm unsure of. I don't know if it was a cop who was showing me this, or if it was a cop chasing the girl."

"Why a cop?"

"Dad, I don't know. *I don't know.* It was just this feeling I had."

"Okay, sport. Remember, nothing to anybody. *Especially* your mother."

Chapter Seven

Several detectives stood by the water fountain in the squad room, laughing. One officer sat at his desk, taking a statement from a homely dressed man that reeked of alcohol.

Richard headed toward Stanley, his ex-partner, sitting alone at his desk, twirling a pencil between his fingers. The relatively handsome and muscular man kept his vigilant concentration on his solo game, unaware of anyone standing beside him. Richard coughed to make his presence known.

"Hey," Stanley said, greeting him with a nod. The pencil fell to the floor. "Damn!"

"Sorry, Stan. Didn't mean to take your focus away from your game." Richard laughed, then stopped when Stan let out a loud 'humph'. "Do you know if the captain's in?"

Scooping the pencil off the floor, Stan leaned back in his chair and looked up, jaw clenched. "No, he left already. Went to see about a case. Should I tell McGuire you were looking for him?"

"No, it's nothing. I'll catch him later." After a slight pause, he asked, "What case?" Richard noted Stanley's hesitation to the question. He worked with him long enough to read him like a book. Stanley would first glance behind him, turn back again, furrowing his brows before one hand went behind his head, scratching at no particular itch.

Richard didn't wait long before Stanley mimicked those exact movements.

"The missing girl from this week."

"He went without me? I'm the investigating officer." *What the hell?* The captain never went solo on an investigation belonging to another detective. Hell, no one did that.

"It was a split-second decision. You were at the hospital, Richard, all night…I guess..."

"Forget it, Stan," he said, anger rising. The captain had undermined and disciplined Stan many times for his short fuse. Richard had felt sorry for the guy. But to have the captain do the same thing to him…he wouldn't stand for it. *He better have a good reason for this.*

"How's Kyle doing? Heard he had a nasty fall and bump to the head."

"He's fine, a slight concussion, that's all." Richard was still pondering why McGuire felt the need to man this investigation on his own. Didn't make sense.

"Did he fall at home or rough playing with his pals?"

"No, he was out at the creek with his friends and stumbled against a boulder. Teens, always exploring and myopic to danger."

"The Creek, eh? Ah, to be young and adventurous again." Stanley sighed, getting up from his desk. "All those young things drooling over our manly hood."

"No, thanks. I'd rather be old and sexually active with my woman."

"Yeah, I guess you're right. It's nice to have a woman whenever you want her, though." Stanley smiled, hips swaying sexually. "Just pick and choose and they come a hoppin' on for the ride…well, that would be my preference, my fantasy at least."

Stan's dry and obnoxious humor was never to Richard's liking. "To each his own, right?"

Stan sat back down, picked up the pencil once more, and twirled. "To each his own, my friend. You're right."

Still reeling with the Captain not calling him to assist in this new disappearance, Richard turned and walked toward the intended destination he was headed to originally.

* * * *

Richard approached Miss Arm Wrestling Champ, Jennifer Akins, sitting at her desk in the godforsaken evidence room. How she could work in this poorly lit, box-infested shack of a place Richard couldn't comprehend. Other than her neat and organized desk, Jennifer's surroundings entailed old filing cabinets of various sizes, some drawers permanently jammed open, their hinges loosely glancing toward the cement floor. The cracked walls needed a good plastering and paint job as well. Nothing compared to the rest of the well-maintained police station above.

"Hey, Jennifer, how's the arm?" Richard asked, pointing to her prized left arm.

Behind her desk hung several Arm-Wrestling awards she won, neatly stacked on a shelf housing her lunch box and a few personal toiletry items she lugged around.

"You wanna have a crack at me?" she dared, positioning for an arm-wrestling match. Her bulging biceps would put any man to shame.

Does she sleep at the gym? "Oh, hell no. All I need is to go home to Susan having to explain a busted arm, from a female, no less."

"Chicken."

"Yep, that's me. Jen, always wanted to ask you a question."

"Fire ahead, chief," she said, and leaned forward, waiting for his question.

"Why do you have those trophies here? Why not have them at home and show them off?"

"Why, that's exactly the reason I have them here, to show them off. Love to see the recruits' expressions when they take a load of my conquests. Puts them in their place right off instead of dreaming off into la-la-land staring at my double D cups." She adjusted her breasts with no shame. "Also, it beats crunching their balls when they try to make a move on me." Big, dark brown eyes lit up as she giggled.

Richard couldn't resist chuckling alongside her. "I knew there was a reason why I liked you. Not for your cup size, but your 'manly' language." Richard glanced toward the cage where old, unsolved case files were neatly locked away. "Jen, I need to check something in the evidence room."

"You know the rules. No signature, no passage."

"Show me the way, dollface," Richard said, signing the evidence log book Jennifer shoved in front of him.

She unlocked the caged screen door. Richard entered and closed it behind him as Jennifer ambled back to her desk.

Walking down several aisles, he scanned through filing cabinets that have seen better days, and boxes. His nerves rattled after fifteen minutes of non-stop searching until he spotted a box against the far wall with the label, CREEK MURDERS–DETECTIVES MCGUIRE AND ANDERSON. His pace hastened. Picking it up, he brought it to the long table at the back of the room. Flipping quickly through some of its paperwork, he picked up the one he was searching for and started to read.

"Two witnesses: Nadine Selleck, 150 Harbour Ridge, and Michelle Hanks, 288 State Ave. Each stated they observed the victims, on the night of their disappearances being picked up by a Caucasian male, age unknown, at the club 'Ecstatica'. Checked up on these leads, but they led to a dead end.

Detective McGuire.

"I don't remember these leads."

Speaking louder than he had intended, Jennifer called out from her desk, "Are we talking to ourselves?"

"As long as I don't answer myself, I'm still sane, Jennifer. No need for a psych evaluation." He let out a fake laugh for her sake.

He wracked his brain for several seconds, trying to bring up any conversation with McGuire that might spark something to recollect these witnesses. Nothing.

Taking out a pad and pen from his jacket, he jotted down the witnesses' information and placed the paper in his pocket.

* * * *

Richard sat on an old broken-down sofa from the sixties, springs poking at his delicate behind. Clothes were strewn all over Nadine Selleck's apartment–one of the witnesses from McGuire's cold case report–amongst the scattered beer bottles lined up like pins in a bowling alley. The ceilings and walls had holes in them; the paint was chipped, hanging like hooks, ready to be pulled. He suppressed an urge to push down on the sofa springs to see if they would bounce back up like a Slinky. Getting one poke up his ass would be–harmful.

The rather haggard-looking brunette sat on the floor that had seen better days, crossed-legged, in torn jeans and an old Harley Davidson T-shirt. She eyed Richard, the cigarette dangling on her cherry lips as she adjusted her bra strap.

"And you are *sure* it was this girl?" he asked, pointing to a photo of one of the missing victims from ten years ago.

Nadine nodded, missing the ashtray and flicking her cigarette on the scratched-up floor.

"How can you be so sure, after all these years?"

"She was young and, by the way she was carrying on in line, I figured it was her first time at a club. She was standing in line, ya' know, outside with a girlfriend, dyke, whatever, and I overheard them talking 'bouts being scared they were gonna be carded. So I told them not to worry…I knew the doorman, stick by me and I'd get them in," Nadine said, handing the photo back to Richard.

"You being such a humanitarian and all," Richard sarcastically spat out, immediately regretting it. His nerves were still bent out of shape with McGuire's need to go out and investigate the latest disappearance without him, plus now finding out about these witnesses he never knew about from their old case.

"Listen, you came to me, remember?" Her slender left hand lifted, index finger pointing toward Richard, jabbed in the air as though making a podium point.

"Sorry, go on." Richard motioned for her to continue. The stench of homemade cigarettes overpowered the claustrophobic room. He wanted to hurry with this interview and get the hell out of there. A wave of nausea began to churn its ugly spell on him, turning his stomach inside out.

Nadine got up and flipped her butt out the window. Leaning against the wall, she continued. "Anyway, the girls were havin' a blast…dancin' and—"

"Drinking, you supplied that, too?" As soon as that unnecessary comment escaped, Richard regretted the sarcastic outburst.

Get a hold of yourself.

She tilted her head, glaring at him. "You know, you're such a funny guy. You think ya know me? What, this dump not to your liking?" Nadine took a couple of steps toward him, wide-eyed, shaking her fist. "What the fuck you know about me?"

That you're an alcoholic and rasp as though you smoke at least five packs a day, but who just might have information for me. "I'm sorry, really, I'm sorry. I promise I won't say anything else." Richard held his hands up in a gesture of surrender.

Nadine rubbed her eyes, scratched her crotch unladylike, then sat back down, leaning against the wall. "Anyway, I noticed this creep…"

Finally. "Why would you define him as a creep?"

"He was too neat–black pants, black shirt, too neat for this club. Everyone came dressed in jeans, casual. This guy was…like callin' for attention, like, 'Hey, Mr. Moneybags here, ladies. Come get some.' So, he approached the girl, whispered something in her ear, she giggled, and out the door they went."

"And you let her?"

"What do I look like, Mother fuckin' Teresa? I helped her get in, that's it. How the fuck did I know she was gonna get killed?"

"Did you get a look at his face?"

"Didn't get up close and personal, ya' know? All I remember are the color of his pants and shirt. Nothin' else. Anyway, I gave this report to some cop, 'bout ten years ago."

"I'm just doing a follow-up," Richard said, the sting of finding out another omission in this investigation by the captain he had once looked up to crawling up his spine.

"Took you long enough." Nadine fished out another cigarette, flicked her lighter, and inhaled before a hoarse cough groaned out of her lips.

Richard figured he wasn't going to get any more information out of her, so he got up to leave. Nadine grunted as she heaved herself off the floor. For a second, it looked as though she was going to accept his extended hand, signaling a courteous goodbye.

Instead, she reciprocated with a, "Yeah, whatever."

Nadine walked him all three steps toward the door.

Walking out, he regretted the way he had spoken to her. "I'm sorry about my comments earlier on."

"Hey, livin' like this, you kinda build a wall to assholes like you," she said, smiling as she slammed the door in his face.

Chapter Eight

Kyle was sprawled on his bed, staring at the ceiling. A sixth sense that he was missing something kept nagging at him.

Shawn sat on the edge of Kyle's desk, fidgeting with his CD player on his lap.

"I have to go back," Kyle suddenly said out of the blue.

"Are you crazy?" Shawn looked stunned, his nostrils flaring like a bull about to charge. He stooped forward, grabbing his CD player just as it was about to fall to the floor.

"I know this intuition is trying to show me something. I can't shake it off," Kyle answered, and sat up. This renewed surge of determination to get to the bottom of this mystery took hold of him. It was like a dark cloud had engulfed him, pushing him to find a way into the clearing. He couldn't forget that girl's sobbing pleas from his vision, begging for her life. He closed his eyes for a split second, shaking his head.

"You're talking crazy, Kyle. You sure that bump on your head didn't loosen some screws?"

"Shawn, I'm telling you, the vision was real. I saw this girl. I could describe to you what she was wearing. She looked scared, *real* scared."

Kyle had played that vision in his head almost every waking moment since his release from the hospital; a dark shadow leaning over an unknown girl, one whose terrified stare etched a horror within Kyle. Then another face would pop up, those same desperate eyes pleading for life. Try as he might, those images haunted him.

Shawn shrugged his shoulders like he gave up trying to change his friend's mind. "Wait till Bradley comes back from the library. Maybe he can make you see the light."

"I'm not waiting. I'm going back now before my mom comes home from shopping," Kyle said and stood up. The urge to investigate further overpowered any rationale in him at the moment. He knew he'd face his parents' wrath if they ever found out. That still didn't sway him from getting ready to go.

"Then I'm a bigger fool than you."

Kyle looked at Shawn, trying to figure out what he meant.

"I'm tagging along in case your ghost friend decides to make you walk the cave ceilings. I'll be there to whack you over the head," Shawn joked. The worried look, however, remained in his eyes.

Kyle smiled. "I think I'm safer with my ghost."

"You think? Your mom finds out and you're...*we're* dead meat. I don't want to be in your shoes, pal. Me, I'll go home and my mom won't even know I've left. If she's sober, well, she might notice," Shawn said, his tone softer, sadder, with the mention of his mom.

"Sorry, man." An image of Shawn's mom sprawled on the living room sofa on one of Kyle's visits sprang to his head. The shades were always pulled to cage any light outside and keep the dark, somber atmosphere within. She was never abusive or anything toward her son, just neglectful, one of the reasons Kyle's and Bradley's parents always allowed him to come over for sleepovers and food.

"Hey, she's a great lady, a heart of gold when sober. Has a drinking problem, that's all. Besides, I'm not missing out on much. I come here, I eat, I sleep, and I get scared out of my wits." Shawn playfully punched Kyle on the arm.

Not knowing what to say to him, Kyle just muttered, "Let's go," and then the two walked out of the bedroom and headed off for the long bus ride and walk to Doorman's Creek.

* * * *

Bradley glanced at his watch as he rang Kyle's doorbell. He took longer than expected, but there were so many files to double-check for any info they might have missed on the Doorman Creek murders. There was nothing more, other than a few clips which he already had, but needed to look over again. Hoping his friends wouldn't be too upset with him being late, he patiently waited as footsteps from within the house sounded.

Seeing Susan at the door surprised him. He was sure Kyle had told him his mom would be gone until supper time.

"Hi, Bradley."

"Hey, Mrs. Anderson. Kyle and Shawn upstairs?"

"No, I thought they were with you at the library, doing some research on visions."

Shit! Bradley tried to cover up somehow. "Um, they probably just went off to the park to play soccer, like we planned. Should have checked there first."

She scrutinized him for several seconds before shaking her head. "Bradley, you're a terrible liar. You guys always play soccer in the daytime. Where are they?" Her sweet greeting features now looked anxious and worried.

He stared anywhere but at Susan, adjusting his glasses nervously. "No, seriously, Mrs. Anderson. They're probably…"

Susan stepped behind the door for a split second, then reappeared with her purse. Taking out her keys, she grabbed Bradley by the shoulder, gently nudging him to the side as she locked the front door.

"Show me this cave, Bradley."

"No, really…" Bradley wasn't even sure if that's where his friends had gone. He prayed they weren't stupid enough to have disobeyed her after she blasted and warned them to stay away from Doorman's Creek. His stomach knotted while he frantically tried to think of a reason to sway Mrs. Anderson to stay home. That's all he needed…to show up at the cave and have Kyle and Shawn beat the crap out of him later.

"I am in no mood, Bradley. My son had a concussion. Now he's hooked on spirits. Show me the way to this cave *now*."

Cornered, with no way out of this mess, he followed her to the car. He couldn't believe his friends had taken off without him. *Serves them right for leaving me behind.*

Susan unlocked the car door for him, and the two drove off toward Doorman's Creek. They sped past her neighborhood. Rows of orderly white clapboard homes, aligned like pages to a book, mirror images of each other; uniformly trimmed green lawns, colorful gardens, similar wooden tole-painted mailboxes. How he wished his insides felt as serene as that picturesque scene. *They're gonna kill me.*

Within twenty minutes or so, and in complete silence other than her exasperated sighs, the car veered off a turn onto a back road leading to Doorman's Creek. Instantly, the crunching of tires over the peppled sideroad hummed its tune.

Bradley was looking out the window when Susan's voice startled him.

"Tell me what happened to Kyle last night."

Bradley didn't know how much Kyle had told his parents and wasn't sure what exactly to reveal. But seeing Susan's anguished face and her tight grip on the steering wheel, he figured lying was out of the question. Besides, if they had waited for him like they were supposed to, he wouldn't be in this situation in the first place.

"We went to the cave because we found a skeleton—"

"What?"

Panic sliced through him. Obviously, Kyle didn't reveal *everything*.

"We found a skeleton the day before, on Saturday…so we, well, I really figured it must be one of the girls who disappeared ten years ago. So we—"

"Why didn't one of you tell us that night?"

"We figured Kyle would."

"Well, he didn't." She tapped the steering wheel hard before turning to her passenger. "We'll find them, then all three of you better tell me everything."

They trailed along a rocky area in the back roads signaling to Bradley they were almost there. As they drew closer, he strained to see ahead in case he spotted his friends. Nothing.

The uncomfortable silence stung him worse than a bee's sting. He realized Mrs. Anderson must have been disappointed in him. It felt as though he inhaled a thick batch of dust, pulverizing his insides by the sudden tightness in his stomach and constricted throat.

Several minutes later, composing himself, Bradley pointed to an opening up ahead. "There, Mrs. A, park over there. We're gonna have to go in Doorman's Creek by foot to get to the cave."

Susan parked by the side of an old dirt road. She looked around her surroundings. Slowly, her angry features changed, eyes narrowed while continuing to scrutinize the area.

"This is the road in my dreams," she mumbled.

Bradley, confused at her soft outburst, followed her out of the car.

"You been here, Mrs. A?"

Susan looked all around, shaking her head. "No, but I've dreamt of this place."

"That's funny cos Kyle, too, has this weird connection to—"

Just then, an unearthly scream broke through the forest, startling them both.

Bradley tore down quickly toward the cave as Susan's footsteps echoed his every step behind him.

Chapter Nine

Richard was heading up the stairs when the doorbell rang. Opening the door, it surprised him to see McGuire standing on his front porch.

"Captain, how are you?"

"Richard." McGuire stood outside, his usual podgy features never revealing his emotions. There could be bombs, a tornado, something going on around him, and the man kept himself in check.

"Something wrong, sir?" Richard asked, curious about this unexpected visit. McGuire had never stepped foot in the Anderson home before, even though he was their neighbor for close to three years.

"No. Stanley mentioned you were looking for me today. I came home early so decided to do the neighborly thing and come here in person."

Richard always got along with the man. He even helped McGuire move his furniture to his new home during a winter storm. The nagging impulse to let McGuire know how pissed off he was about investigating the latest disappearance without him suddenly came to the forefront. *Let it go, man.*

"No, it was nothing. My son…here, got a minute?" Richard asked.

"Sure."

He moved to the side and allowed McGuire to enter.

The captain sat on the living room sofa while Richard seated himself in the armchair. McGuire's eyes flitted around the room, nervously. He cocked his head left and right as though cracking ailing joints, rubbing his palms together.

"We've got the same layout except our dining room is in a separate room."

"So was ours, but Susan wanted an open concept, so down came the wall."

"I've been thinking of remodeling, just haven't had the time yet. Can't believe we've been here almost three years, and this is the first time I've stepped into your home."

"Never too late, right? We'll arrange a barbeque and have you and your son over."

McGuire just nodded.

After several awkward, silent seconds, Richard asked, "Coffee?"

"No, thank you. You started to say something about Kyle?"

"My son, last night in the hospital, started ranting about our old case, the Doorman murders. He wasn't making much sense at the beginning but began describing the murders like he knew what he was talking about," Richard said, gathering his thoughts on how much to reveal without allowing anger to choke him again.

"How could he? He's only, what, fifteen?"

"Exactly. His friend, Bradley, on the other hand, is a fanatic about trying to puzzle out murders so, at first, I figured, because of the bump he sustained, he might have been relating things Bradley might have said or read to him at one time or another."

"You don't believe that now?" He aimed a persistent stare at Richard.

"No, because he mentioned the bite marks on the girls' necks, along with the fact they were both topless, which we never revealed to the public."

"How would he know this?" McGuire cocked his head again to the side, reminding Richard how similar to a bulldog his captain really resembled. All the "Bulldog Cap'n" jokes at the precinct came fluttering through him. He suppressed the urge to snigger.

"Captain, I know this is going to sound crazy, but he, at one point, looked at me and, I swear, he had that same firmness old man Doorman had when we questioned him."

"So, what was it you wanted me for at the precinct?" He pulled his gaze away from Richard for a split second before staring back at him.

The subtle change in the discussion didn't escape Richard. "Well, I looked back at the files…" *Be calm now.* Nerves were twitching to come out and bluntly ask why the hell McGuire took off this morning without him.

"You did?"

Richard nodded, spotting a slightly uncomfortable shifting in the captain's body language. "And I noticed there were two leads never followed up on." *Why are you so nervous, Cap?*

"Really?" McGuire leaned forward in his seat.

Are you squirming over the Doorman case or worried I'm going to blast you about today's lone investigation?

"There were two witnesses who said each victim, before they went missing, met up with a guy from the same club, Ecstatica."

"How do you know this?"

"I went and found one of the witnesses and questioned her. The funny thing is, she said she spoke to someone about this, and I assume you because I wasn't even aware of the girls' existence." Richard studied his captain's face for any sign of guilt. Other than one chubby hand rubbing his scruffy chin in thought, the cap gave nothing away.

"You know, you're right. I remember now. Nothing ever panned out from it, though. Couldn't trace anything back to this guy. Not enough information other than what he wore, I believe. Besides those two witnesses, nothing else." There was a brief, awkward pause. "You know, Richard, I'll have that coffee now, if you don't mind."

Richard wasn't too keen about the switch in topics from McGuire, and made a mental note to pursue this further. "Sure thing, Cap. I'll be right back."

He started toward the kitchen but eyed McGuire getting up, pacing back and forth a couple of times.

"You take sugar and milk?"

"Two sugars, no milk. Where's your son now?" McGuire called out as Richard disappeared into the kitchen.

"Beats me. Out with his friends, I guess."

McGuire patted his gun in his holster as he walked into the kitchen.

"I was going to bring our coffee out to the living room. You didn't have to come in here."

"I'm sorry, Richard."

* * * *

McGuire stepped out of the Anderson home, glancing about before redirecting his focus back to the main door.

"Okay, Richard, I'll see you later. Thanks for the coffee and the discussion. Appreciate your understanding." He leaned forward, grabbed a hold of the handle, and shut the Anderson's front door.

As he headed down the driveway, he spotted old Mrs. Druid sitting on her front porch, across the street.

He waved to her just before he unlocked his front door and walked in.

* * * *

Susan and Bradley raced through the forest toward the scream that broke the silence just a moment ago.

"Kyle?" Susan frantically called out her son's name several more times. "Bradley, do you see anything?"

"Nothing. Kyle! Shawn!"

Susan distinctly heard the faint rustling of footsteps trampling toward them. From the distance, she spotted Shawn running, every so often looking over his shoulder. Every leg muscle ached as her feet bolted forward.

"He's…he's gone crazy…we were standing by—" Shawn sputtered, in-between deep breaths, hands waving all over the place. Blood oozed from his arms that had long slashes, most likely scraped against trees as he ran.

"Shawn!" Susan grabbed a hold of him, shaking him. "Shawn, where's Kyle?"

Shawn looked behind and pointed, fighting hard for breath. “I-It’s not Kyle, Mrs. A. It’s old man Doorman.”

Susan glared at the teen before releasing him and brushed past him, running in the direction he came from. Bradley stayed behind with his friend, who was barely keeping his fear contained.

From behind, Shawn continued to yell, “It’s old man Doorman! He’s got Kyle!”

She doubled her pace, frantically searching for any sign where this cave could be. Several squirrels scurried up branches, grunting their annoyance at her for disturbing them. Consumed with fear, she jumped over fallen branches, propelling forward as though in a race for her life…her *son’s* life.

Susan spotted the cave’s opening to her right and rushed in, tripping on a rock. Getting up, she swiped at the blood oozing from a gash just below her knee.

“Kyle? Kyle, where are you?” Eyes focused all around trying to adjust to the dim lighting.

“Help me.” A raspy, low-pitched voice sounded about a few yards further in.

Her head jerked up, and she scrambled in that direction toward the faint light illuminating up ahead. Kyle stood with his back to her, body rigid. Slowly, he turned around and faced her, moving in an almost sleep-walking state.

“Help...me!” came out of Kyle’s mouth, but it wasn’t his voice.

Susan froze mid-stride. “Kyle?” She approached him, terrified, remembering what Shawn kept yelling. *“It’s not Kyle. It’s old man Doorman.”* Her son was looking straight at her with glazed-over eyes. That deep voice caused goosebumps to rise all over her body.

"Kyle, it's me, mom."

"Find c…cop," Kyle muttered in a zombie state of being.

"Who are you!? Leave my son *alone*!" Susan reached forward, grabbed a hold of Kyle, and hugged him in a tight embrace.

A sudden cool breeze whisked by her just as Kyle slumped in her arms.

"Bradley! Shawn!"

* * * *

The nurse behind the desk handed Susan the telephone again. She'd forgotten her cell at home. Trying to control the trembling in her hands, she dialed home.

"Where are you, Richard?" she said out loud, glancing at her watch. Richard should have been home by now. Susan dialed a couple of times more before giving up.

She turned to look at Shawn, who sat on the bench outside Kyle's hospital room. His hands were clasped behind his head, leaning back against the wall, eyes closed. He looked exhausted, his clothes muddied and torn, blood on his arms now dried up. Shawn had ridden in the ambulance with Kyle while Susan dropped Bradley off at his home before heading off to the hospital herself.

"Mrs. Anderson?"

Susan spun around, startled at the doctor's gentle touch on her shoulder.

"Yes. How is he?" She drew in a sharp breath, hoping for good news.

"He's doing fine. His breathing has gone back to normal. We'd like to keep him overnight, however, for observation. With his concussion from the night before, we just want to monitor him. You better go home, though. You look worse than he does. Would you like me to check that cut on your knee?" He pointed at the dried blood glued like paper mâché around her knee.

Susan shook her head, rubbing her forehead to keep a migraine at bay.

"I'll call you at home if anything comes up, Mrs. Anderson. I don't expect any upsets tonight. He's resting comfortably."

"Thank you for everything, Dr. Katz." They shook hands, then watched him walk down the corridor. Tired and upset that Richard didn't answer her phone calls, she figured he must have been called to the station. She'd call him at the office if he wasn't home by the time she got there.

Gently, not to frighten him, she nudged Shawn's shoulder.

"Let's go, Shawn. I'll take you home. Doc said Kyle's going to be fine."

"No, he isn't." He leaned forward, looking up. "That wasn't Kyle, I tell you. Old man Doorm—" Shawn blurted, wiping beads of sweat around his forehead. He wore a pained expression, eyes wide, glimpses of tears forming.

Susan lifted a finger to her lips to quiet him. "Keep your voice down," she warned, staring across toward the nurses' station to make sure no one heard his outburst. The last thing she needed was for someone to think her son *and* his friend were off their rocker, or worse, taking drugs.

She motioned for Shawn to follow her outside. He sluggishly rose to his full height, taking a last look toward Kyle's hospital door before walking off with Susan.

The air had turned crisp compared to the warmth that tilled the earth earlier. A faint breeze kissed her exposed skin, sending chills over her body as they stepped out of the hospital. These chills didn't compare to the extreme goosebumps she experienced seeing her son possessed. Susan tried to push that image out of her head, but the coincidence with the dirt road in Doorman's Creek and the one constantly following her in every dream was too much to handle right now.

"Shawn, I want you to tell me exactly what happened," Susan said, approaching the car.

"We…no, Kyle said he needed to go back. He said he felt it was necessary. Kept insisting something was drawing him to the cave."

"What, do you know?"

"He felt…I don't know. He said he saw a vision of a girl being chased by someone."

"Today?" Susan was confused. Was Shawn referring to the episode from Saturday or today?

They stepped into the car, and she started the engine.

"Shawn, Kyle's vision of a girl was from today?" she repeated, needing to put all the pieces together.

"No, the first time, Saturday. We were standing, about to dig… and then out of the blue, Kyle starts shaking like… like a seizure or something. Bradley and I went up to him and he pushed us away. Not softly, Mrs. A. He *really* pushed us away with tremendous force, barely touching us. Then he went blank. Just staring out into nothing. The next thing we know, he falls and hits his head on a boulder. Bradley and I carried him up to the back roads and flagged someone down. That's when we called you on the guy's cell."

"What about today, Shawn?" Bradley had already filled her in on most of Saturday's happenings. She needed to discover today's occurrence and make some sense of it.

Shawn turned to face her, pallid and scared.

"It wasn't the same. As soon as we got into the cave, he complained about the stench. But there was no smell. I told him so. But he kept insisting he could smell it."

"There was nothing?"

Shawn vehemently shook his head. "We started walking farther till we reached the spot…" Shawn fell quiet for a moment.

"Please, go on." Susan needed to hear what had freaked Shawn out. As crazy as it sounded, she had come up with her conclusion, certain it was identical to his.

"Kyle was standing by the skeleton we discovered and then turned to ask if I felt that."

"Felt what?"

"I don't know…he was talking about the cold wind, breeze, whatever, but again, there was no wind, there was no breeze like there was no smell!" Shawn slumped back in his seat.

Susan remembered that cold sensation just before Kyle passed out in her arms, a deathly chill as though touched from beyond the grave. She wanted to pull back and stop her inquisition, seeing how upset Shawn was, but the need to know everything overpowered her. "What happened next?"

"He started having that seizure thing again. He turned around and…and I swear, Mrs. A., I swear his face looked at me but he looked like…like old man Doorman."

Her heart hammered against her chest. She, too, had the oddest feeling the voice coming out of her son sounded exactly like Doorman. She had met the man on several occasions in passing while out on errands or with Kyle. And to have Shawn come to the same conclusion, in some odd way, secured she wasn't going out of her mind.

"I'm serious," Shawn continued in a rant. "He appeared like the retard for an instant. I'm sorry…I should have stayed, but I…I got scared."

"He wasn't a retard, Shawn. The man was homeless and had a stutter. And there's nothing to be sorry about. I understand why you got scared. Does anyone else know about this?" *God, I hope not.*

"Who the hell would believe me?" His tone was thick with anguish. He leaned his head back against the seat, eyes closing.

Sympathizing, she was able to relate to this craziness. Her only obstacle now was how to convince Richard about her dreams and Kyle's intuition connection.

Shortly, they arrived at Shawn's house.

Closing the passenger door, Shawn leaned in the passenger window and stared at her. "Something possessed Kyle. I know this," he said, then took off toward his home's unlit porch.

He was right, and she knew it, although it didn't make sense how that was possible. The bigger and more disturbing question was, why? Why Kyle?

Susan waited until he was safely inside before she continued her drive home.

* * * *

"Richard? I'm home. And you left the front door unlocked. Nice going, officer."

She placed her keys on the hall table, then turned to find Richard and clue him in on Kyle's newest mishap. About to take a step, her gaze landed in the living room. Pillows scattered everywhere, the lamp lay smashed on the beige rug, and paintings hung sideways.

"Richard!" She yelled his name one more time before running out of the house.

He had drilled into her enough times to know to get out as quickly as possible if she ever came home and thought someone burglarized the house.

Afraid someone might still be inside, she crouched low, edging around the outside of their stone and brick house, peeking inside the windows. Careful not to make any noise, she inched her way around the rose bushes, the hibiscus plants, securing her balance by lightly touching the outer walls.

Once outside the kitchen window, she stood on her tippy toes and carefully looked inside.

God, what if someone's still inside? She cursed softly for leaving her purse and not grabbing her cell from inside the main foyer.

Bravely, she poked her head as close to the window as she dared to peer inside. The light coming in from the hallway lit just enough to make out the inside of the kitchen. Her first glance concentrated on any shadows moving in the hallway, then she slowly scanned the area, gazing from the counter to the floor. At that moment, her emotions were ripped apart…Richard was sprawled on the tiled floor in a pool of blood.

Without thinking, Susan backtracked toward the front of the house. Oblivious to anything in her path, she trampled over her pride flowerbed, and stumbled across the garbage bin Richard was to have placed back in the garage. Getting up dazed, her squeals for help cut through the night air as she rushed toward the kitchen.

"Oh, my God! Richard!!" Sobs tore from her as she knelt beside him, checking his pulse.

"NO!!"

Susan cradled him in her arms, rocking back and forth, oblivious to the sirens and flashing lights streaming through the windows.

Chapter Ten

The distinct clicking of her bedroom door opening caught her attention, but Susan lay still. Every ounce of energy, that spark that made her feel as though she could accomplish anything she set her mind on, drained from her spirit three weeks ago when Richard died. The only thing she could muster lately was to get up, retrieve aspirin from the medicine cabinet, pop a couple of them every so often, then pretend to clean the house before retreating to her bedroom. She barely remembered the last time a full meal was prepared. All she could do was crumple under her bedsheets and hope to wake up from this nightmare.

"Mom? You awake?" Kyle's voice rang softly, almost in a whisper.

Susan forced herself to turn and face him. Drumming up the energy to rise out of bed scaled at the hard level lately.

"Kyle? I'm sorry, sweetie, I'll get up and make us some lunch."

"No, mom, that's okay. I just wanted to let you know the man is here from the Salvation Army to pick up Dad's… pick up Dad's clothes."

She had procrastinated as long as she could, keeping Richard's scent in his clothes close to her. Each whiff inhaled augmented sweet memories, making it almost bearable if only to hold on to those images for a while. Yet with each passing day, that procrastinating selfishness hurt Kyle, seeing his dad's belongings in boxes smack in the middle of the hallway.

Her robe lay by the red velvet chair near the dresser. Forcing herself up, she put it on, ambled toward the opened window, and peered outside. The sun blared down on her cheeks, but she paid it no attention. Her focus rested on the children playing on their front lawns.

She recalled and captured Richard's smile when Kyle was born.

"What shall I do, mom?"

Susan slowly turned, avoiding direct eye contact. She stared beyond, at the opened door behind Kyle. "Tell him… I'll bring it to them later."

She stared at her son. Kyle's somber mood resembled hers lately. She knew she had to snap out of this gripping stupor but just couldn't shake it. The zest for life was gone; that joy that always pushed her forward died the day they buried Richard. But seeing Kyle's dark circles under his eyes hurt her immensely. She vowed today would be different.

Kyle left, and she walked over to her bureau, picking up a picture she had taken with Richard at the annual police picnic last year. They both donned baby bonnets as a joke when they refused to participate in some of the races. Those were the rules. Participate or be considered babies. Babies it was, and they had spent the rest of the afternoon underneath a tree, with a blanket and picnic basket filled with goodies, along with a bottle of white wine.

Fighting back tears, Susan cradled the picture close to her heart, that longing to have him wrap his arms around her stirring once more. All those dreams and plans about what they'd do once he retired, gone.

"Oh, sweetie, I miss you so much."

With every bit of energy she could muster, she dressed and headed toward Richard's study. She had left this room untouched; never stepped inside until today. She'd deal with the boxes filled with most of his clothing later. Right now, she needed to busy herself.

The mahogany desk oozed with Richard's personae, punctuating the longing to have him by her side once more. Fingers gently patted the top of the smooth surface, imagining him sitting back as he always did, smiling at her and motioning to her to sit on his lap. She shook her head vigorously, erasing the picture, and continued her intended coping mechanism—dusting.

Opening one drawer to sort out his papers, she immediately slammed it shut, plopping down hard on his chair. With her head resting on the desk, the floodgates opened, releasing all pent-up sorrow and anger. Nothing else disturbed the silence other than uncontrollable sobbing.

After several minutes, she eased back against the chair, wiped away fallen tears, and stood. Dusting would wait for another day.

Reaching around the door to get to the light switch, she spotted one of Richard's jackets hanging on a hook. Caressing it to her face, the woodsy scent of his cologne still lingered. With new tears held at bay, she patted the jacket as though ironing out invisible wrinkles. As she did, a piece of paper sticking out of a pocket caught her attention. Reaching inside, she removed the paper and read it.

'It seems strange that both witnesses mentioned Ecstatica. Ask Captain about it. Nadine Towers 331-4397 and Susan Zimmerman 582–6161. Nadine said cop took her statement ten years ago.'

With the note shoved into her back pocket, she headed back to his desk. She flipped through his agenda, looking at every written detail for clues on what Richard may have been working on when her gaze wandered to an entry from the Saturday Kyle was first hospitalized.

'Ask Kyle the exact whereabouts of the skeleton.'

"Kyle! Kyle!" With a trembling hand, she pushed loose hair away from her face. A sudden weight of questions filled her mind.

"Yeah, mom?" Kyle answered from somewhere upstairs.

"Come in the study for a sec."

In no time at all, he entered, staring at her.

"Kyle, you mentioned to your father about the remains you found?"

He nodded.

"When?"

"The night of my concussion, the first time at the hospital."

"What did he say?"

"Nothing. I told him we had found this human skeleton and that…and I told him about this…vision I had." Kyle hesitated, shuffling his feet back and forth, his concentration focused everywhere else except on his mother.

"Did he believe you?"

He looked lost in her line of questioning.

"Kyle, look at me. Did he believe you?" she repeated, growing anxious by the second.

Kyle snapped his head up and stared at her.”Not at first. He probably figured I got knocked real hard. Why? You okay, mom?”

She ignored his questions. “What did you say that made him change his mind?”

“What do you mean?” He stopped the insistent shuffling.

“Kyle, you must have said something to him that made him believe you.”

“I don’t know.”

“Kyle, *please*, try to remember.” For some odd reason, that piece of paper and its scribbling woke up something inside her, and she finally felt like a woman with a purpose. She was eager to shed the zombie inhabiting her body these past three weeks. But where she was heading with this line of questioning remained unclear, even to her. Just working on an instinct, a hunch, something that instantly pushed her to gather information.

“I don’t know, mom. I don’t remember.”

Kyle’s shoulders hunched forward, his head bent down, shaking left to right. Guilt and grief gnawed at her for making him go through this, but she needed answers, so the drilling continued.

“I’m sorry, sweetheart, but up till now, I had no clue your dad knew about your find.”

“I didn’t know *you* knew?” he said, sounding surprised.

“Shawn told me everything the night I brought him home from the hospital. The day your father...” She paused, a heavy sigh exhaled, lips quivering. “Kyle, please, sit down. This is very important. I want to know exactly what you said to your father.”

Kyle sat on the chair in front of the desk and recounted his experience the best he could.

"How do you know it was the creek and someone was chasing this girl in your vision?"

"She ran past this tree we nicknamed the Dinosaur Tree. You know, Dad asked me the same thing. You two think… thought alike."

Susan sat on the desk in front of Kyle, taking his hand in hers. Her heart ached to put him through this recollection. If Richard's death had anything to do with one of his old cases, she had to find out. Her constant dreams, Kyle's pull to the Creek...that wasn't and *couldn't* be a coincidence.

"Go on." She took a settling breath.

"Then, it changed."

"What changed?" She bit her lower lip trying to contain anxious nerves.

"My vision. All of a sudden, I see that girl lying next to another girl, in blue jeans, dead."

"Is this everything you told your dad?"

Kyle blinked several times before shaking his head. "I mentioned they had no tops on, and bite marks on their necks, and…yeah, that's when Dad freaked out."

"Why? What did he say?"

"He told me not to mention this to anyone because these were details the police never revealed to reporters."

"I have a gut feeling your father wasn't killed because of a blotched-up robbery like Captain McGuire reported." That analysis stretched far and wide in her mind. The screams of the sirens the night Richard died, the living room's upheaval, the blood, and his body...all rushed forward. No, she brushed aside the initial report, intuition dictating her current hunch was right. Richard was murdered. But *why* was the million-dollar question?

"Mom, now that we're discussing visions, please, tell me about the dream you kept having back then."

"It doesn't matter. My dream stopped the day your dad died." Susan tried to get up and walk away, but Kyle placed his hand in front of her, preventing her from leaving.

His eager, inquisitive eyes met hers, and she clearly saw the pleading in them. "It does, to me. Please."

She nodded. "I kept dreaming of this…Dr. Death character," she began, her somber voice slow-paced as though searching for the right words, "I would describe to your father…standing by an ambulance, smiling at me."

"That means a warning of something about to happen."

"How do you know?"

"The project…last year? About dreams? I worked for three months on it. I studied so many dream interpretations."

"I wish I said something earlier, maybe all this…"

Kyle rose and hugged her.

"It's none of our faults, Mom. Would you have believed me if I told you about this wacky connection to the Creek? I don't think so unless you actually witnessed whatever possessed me as you did."

They cried, huddled together for several minutes before Susan gently pushed him to the side, gazing at him proudly. She stood from the desk with a newfound strength missing for a while now.

"Kyle, listen to me. I want you, Bradley, and Shawn to gather up any info on these Doorman Creek murders you can find. Try to be inconspicuous."

"Okay, but why?"

"Like I said, I have a gut feeling this Doorman Creek cold case and current disappearances tie in with your dad's death somehow. And I want to find out. Your father left the morning he died telling me he was going to follow up on some leads about the Creek killings. I didn't think much of it then until I spotted a note in his agenda, and now you confirmed talking to him about them."

"You think he found something out?"

Susan took out the scrap piece of paper she retrieved from Richard's jacket and stared at it.

"I'm going to find out."

* * * *

The air was hazy with all the cigarette smoke fogging up the station outside. Civilians, cops, and most likely lawyers, standing, chatting, talking about cases and whatnots. The distinct mix of cigar and Marlboro weaving through the air nauseated her. Pushing past them, she hurried up the stairs and made her way inside.

Susan stood by the precinct's double doorway trying to find a familiar face. Several cops walked past, paying no attention to her. She bypassed everyone, weaving in and out, unsure who was a criminal and who was an undercover cop. Some were easier to spot than others; the clanging of their handcuffs tightly secured around their wrists as they professed their innocence helped to sort them out. She climbed the in-badly-need-of-some-paint stairs to the first floor…Richard's floor.

The familiarity of this area, along with faces she had met at one police function or the other, calmed her somewhat. Glancing about, beginning to quench that upset in her stomach, Susan felt an enormous pang ripple her insides, letting out a heavy sigh.

She spotted Richard's desk, the memorable clutter of papers and pictures of his family now gone. As though the man never existed...

Approaching her was a familiar face. Tall, short brown hair, a clean-shaven face, and a smile that warmed her heart.

"Mrs. Anderson, how are you?" the man greeted.

"Hi, Phil, how are you?".

He leaned forward and gave her a tight embrace. "I made detective," he said, extending his chest, and showing off his badge.

"Oh, I'm so happy for you. Richard would have been proud of you."

"I'm so sorry. I still can't believe he's gone." Phil's kind and sincere face made her feel uncomfortable. She didn't come to the precinct searching for pity; she came for answers.

"He meant a lot to me. If it weren't for him, I would never have made it to detective."

That was her man, always helping others succeed if they deserved it and worked hard to achieve it. Richard had specifically taken a liking to Phil, inviting him over several times for supper to coach him wherever help was needed.

Wanting to leave this hurtful memory behind, she changed the subject.

"Do you know if Stan is around?" She glanced around, spotting Richard's ex-partner by his desk. "Never mind, I see him. Good luck, Phil, and please, keep in touch."

Phil leaned forward, hugging her once again. "If *ever* you need something, give me a call."

"Thank you." His sincerity touched her, but before he could make further comments on how he missed Richard, she turned away. Shrugging off the melancholic emotion, she headed in Stan's direction.

He looked surprised when he glanced up from his desk. "Susan. What a surprise. How are you?"

"Hi, Stan. Not bad. Could be better, though." Wringing her hands, she gave a quick look over her shoulder. "Can we go somewhere to speak in private?"

"We have nothing new on Richard's case, I'm afraid. We've been working round the clock on this one. I promise you we'll catch the person who did this." His fist thumped hard against the desk. Several people close by turned to stare before going back to their business.

"No, it's something else I want to talk to you about."

Stan stood, gently placed his hand on her shoulder, and escorted her to the room off to the side, the only free interrogation room.

"What's up?" Stan closed the door and then sat at the far corner by the table, while Susan stood, restlessly playing with her fingers. There was an unbroken current of hope she prayed would not end up with disappointment at the end of this visit.

There was a slight hesitation for a second, unsure of where to begin. She tried to calm the emotions smothering her at the moment, feeling almost like a caged animal wanting to free itself from isolation. "Stan, can you tell me what Richard was working on before his death?"

Stan ogled her, his left brow lifting quizzically. "Why?"

"Please, just amuse me."

Stan released a low grunt, unamused. "Well, the only case he was involved with full time was that missing girl."

"Was he following up on anything the morning he got killed?"

Stan stood and ambled around the table toward her. His right index finger touched his temple in a circular motion, shaking his head.

"I remember him asking to see the captain, but I told him he was out on a case. Actually, *their* case." He went on giving her the details of that day, the way Richard became upset with McGuire.

With a determined step, she neared him.

"Does the name Ecstatica mean anything to you?" Her voice a mere whisper, Susan searched his face for any recollection spurred by the name of the club.

Stan thought about it, then shook his head. "Should it?"

"I thought it might have something to do with the Doorman Creek murders."

"The captain's and Richard's old cold case? That's had a headstone for quite some time, with no leads."

"Can I ask you for a favor? Can you look up Richard's files on those murders to see if Ecstatica is mentioned anywhere for me?"

"I don't know." Stan walked away from her, shaking his head, a stark contrast to his welcoming stance earlier on.

A shadow of despair drowned her hopes at that point. "Please, Stan, it's important to me."

"All the Doorman files are in the evidence room downstairs. Susan, you're asking a lot from me here." His gaze darted around the room before landing back on her. "The cap finds out I'm handing out info to a civilian, it's gonna be my hide, you know that, right?" After a minute of silence, he walked away, opened the door, then turned around. "Okay, wait here. Let me see what I can find out for you. You're gonna owe me big time."

"You're a doll." A release of anxiety exited an overly exhausted body. *Finally, I'm getting somewhere.*

Stan gave her a wink and immediately closed the door behind him.

He was headed for the staircase when he bumped into Captain McGuire.

"Stan, did you see Susan Anderson? Phil said she was here just a while ago." McGuire glanced about.

"She's in the interrogation room by the side entrance. Poor thing, she's grasping at anything to figure out Richard's death."

Captain McGuire ignored Stan, walked right past him, and headed toward the interrogation room.

Stan muttered, "Asshole," then stomped away quickly.

Susan, deep in thought on Richard's last few days, was startled when the door swung open suddenly. Her hopes of Stan walking in with some news for her quickly washed away. McGuire stepped in, donning a distinct scowl etched on his features.

"Captain McGuire, so nice to see you." She tried to keep the edginess out of her tone.

"Susan. How are you and Kyle doing?"

His pretentious stance for small talk irked her. *How did he know I was here?*

"We're fine." Anxiety built, worried Stan might show up while McGuire remained here with her. The reason as to why she came to the station reaching McGuire made her jumpy. Until she had proof to show him and demand why he initially marked Richard's case as a botched burglary attempt, she was going to keep quiet.

He approached her, meaty fingers pulling her closer to give her a friendly peck on the cheek.

"How's Lewis?" she asked, taking a step back, distancing herself from him. She needed to keep her guard up. Sooner or later, the question of why she came here was inevitably going to spring up, there was no doubt in her mind. The Captain, according to Richard's caricature of him in the past, warned her he wasn't a man for idle chit-chat without a purpose.

"He's okay. At his age, you'd figure he'd watch out for himself. But, I have to nag him to take those pills. The only person he'd listen to with no arguments was his mom, God rest her soul."

Susan, Richard, and Kyle had attended Margaret McGuire's funeral two years ago. Only fifty, yet an aneurism doesn't care what age you are. She died right after supper, sitting at the table, laughing with her husband and son one minute, then dead the next.

"Can't the doctor intervene, stress the importance?" She needed to keep the conversation away from today's visit.

"Trust me, he has. Lewis feels great so he figures he can stop them, but I tell him, along with Dr. Sugarman, that it's a chemical imbalance and without his meds, he'll go back to his old mood swings."

"Kids. The things we do for them." *Please leave before Stan gets back.*

"And you, Susan, how are you managing these days?"

An ominous feeling swept through her. Both arms wrapped around her upper torso as though warming a cool breeze. She looked up at him, trying to decide how much to reveal.

"Surviving." Instinct dictated to divulge nothing.

"You know, I talked to Richard the day he…well…"

"Really?" In the blink of an eye, she wanted to spill her guts but refrained.

Something still nagged her about him, and until this sensation went away, there was no way she would reveal anything.

"I was doing a follow-up on a case we were working on that morning."

"The missing girl?"

"That's right. I guess Richard must have discussed a lot of our cases with you." His eyes bore into her.

"Not really. That was one thing he was adamant about. No business at home."

"Oh." There was a slight, uncomfortable pause. "Has Kyle had any more visions?"

Startled by that revelation, the knot in her stomach tightened like a coil. "You know about them?" She wanted his help, yet that nagging presence about him prodded her to continue vigilant secrecy.

"Richard told me about them that same morning." She was shocked Richard never mentioned anything, then realized he never had a chance. "No. Kyle's doing fine."

"Is there a reason you're here? Can I help you with something?"

Here we go.

"No. I just…I just wanted to see some familiar faces, that's all." She realized how stupid that statement sounded…see familiar faces while holed up in the interrogation room. *Nice comeback, idiot.*

"You're always welcomed here, Susan, you know that. Being neighbors and all, I can pass by, see if there's anything I can do for you, around the house."

"That's kind of you, Captain."

"Mike, Susan, no Captain. I thought we were friends. Every time you call me Captain, I feel ten times my age and not fifty-five."

"All right...Mike. I better be going. Kyle probably is wondering where I went."

"If Kyle has any more dreams, let me know. The kid might be psychic. Could help us with the Doorman case. In any other circumstance or person, I'd laugh off psychics and their premonitions, but, well, I have a feeling Kyle's different."

Sly devil.

A nervous laugh escaped her lips. "I seriously doubt that."

McGuire gently placed his arm around her shoulder and led her out of the interrogation room.

"It was nice seeing you, Susan. I'll keep in touch."

Susan reciprocated his friendly peck on the cheek and left. Almost at the bottom of the staircase, she bumped into Stan.

Holding on to his arm, she asked, "Was there anything about Ecstatica?" The question was rushed, hoping to get answers in case the captain came their way.

"It's a nightclub downtown."

"Does it mention Richard talking to any witnesses?"

"There was a mention the captain followed up, but it led to a dead end." He stared at her for a second, thumb rubbing against his badge. "I need to ask you again why the interest now?"

"Richard's death was marked as a botched robbery, yet nothing was taken."

"He most likely interrupted the perp."

"Stan, please. Someone killed Richard with plenty of time to grab valuables according to the time of death. No, I'm sure this wasn't a robbery attempt but something connected to the Doorman case."

"Listen, I'm still technically on desk duty, but if you need my help with anything else, don't hesitate to call. In the meantime, I'll try to see what I can find out on this end for you."

"Thank you, Stan."

"Anytime, Susan. Always willing to help a damsel in distress, you know that. Was there anything else?"

"No. Just a curiosity I had to clear, that's all." Susan glanced up and caught McGuire at the top of the staircase staring at them as she hugged Stan goodbye. There was a dark glint in the captain's eyes she didn't like.

* * * *

On his way back to his office, McGuire spotted Stan heading toward his desk. Upping his pace, he reached over and clutched Stan's arm as he was about to sit.

"Stan, Susan okay? She looks frail."

"She's doing fine, Cap, considering she lost her husband. She was just curious about the Doorman files and the club Ecstatica."

"And?" McGuire lowered his voice, looking over his shoulder toward the occupied desks.

Stan nudged his arm free from the tight grasp before responding. "Nothing. I told her it was a dead end. After all, no leads were ever followed upon, nothing concluded, right? Dead end, like I told her."

"You shouldn't be discussing cases with her or any civilian. Have you forgotten you're still on desk duty for another week?" His detective's foolhardy action openly exasperated McGuire. But more so, by his insinuation and emphasis on "no leads" and "dead end." There *was* one suspect according to the captain's gut feeling but no tangible evidence to connect the perp, and McGuire had swallowed his pride then, but that case never left him entirely.

"I just felt sorry for her, thought it–"

"Never mind." McGuire rolled his right shoulder and took a deep breath, trying to control a fit of anger flaring up.

"But, Cap—"

"Stan, your anger management classes working okay? Teaching you anything? I'd hate to see your evaluation asking for another month just sitting by a desk."

Stan stared at him without saying a word, then sat by his desk.

McGuire turned and entered his office.

* * * *

Susan whiffed the crisp air that blew in from her car window. The breeze helped clear her head. All she craved was to head home, get in the tub and soak her problems away with some lavender bath balms, and a lot of soap bubbles. This enticing thought came to an abrupt end.

Kyle, Shawn, and Bradley were sitting by the steps of the house. By the tense expressions on their faces, Susan couldn't distinguish if they were holding good news or news to rile her headache even further. They immediately stood when she pulled into the driveway and parked the car.

"Mom, Mom, you gotta hear this," Kyle called out before she had a chance to step out of the car. Susan could tell by Kyle's borderline hysteria he had something really important to tell her. He kept pointing to his tape recorder held tightly against his chest with one hand. He reminded her of a wild barbarian, sword held tightly against his body, ready to strike at his foe.

"What? Did you guys find out anything new?" Susan asked, locking the car door.

Shawn and Bradley were also visibly excited by the news Kyle was eager to share. They kept shifting from one position to another like they had ants in their pants as she approached them.

"No way," Shawn exclaimed, his eyes almost popping out of their sockets. "We *heard* something new."

"What are you talking about?" Susan asked, puzzled. She glanced from one boy's enthusiastic and gleaming grin to the next.

"Here, listen to this." Kyle's finger was poised over the tape recorder's ON button when Susan stopped him.

"Hold on, guys, let's go inside." She glanced across the lawn to the McGuire home, where Lewis, the captain's son, sat outside on his lawn chair, tanning.

From the boys' jubilant behavior, she realized privacy is what they needed. Although Lewis appeared oblivious to their presence, she wanted to be sure nothing would be overheard.

Susan unlocked the door and marched right in, straight to the kitchen, placing her bag on the counter. The boys' heavy footfalls followed right behind.

Sitting down, she motioned for them to take a seat at the table. Kyle sat while Shawn and Bradley eagerly paced back and forth, satisfied smiles on both of them.

"Okay, Mom, we were at Bradley's, looking over some newspaper clippings he has when we remembered the tape recorder."

"What about it?" Susan asked, confused, staring at the recorder in Kyle's hands.

"When we went back to the cave the second time—" Kyle began.

Bradley butted in, "We thought we'd tape our discovery. Something like a play by play, you know, so we can have evidence of our find."

"Anyway," Kyle picked up the story, "we had forgotten about it, till today." His blue eyes sparkled with excitement.

"I wanted to tape—" Shawn began.

"So," Kyle interrupted, "we rewound the tape to where we had left off and that's when we heard it."

"Heard what? You're not making any sense!" Susan was molested by confusion, trying to sort out what they were talking about. "You took this tape recorder and…?"

"Listen," Kyle said and pressed play, beginning with Bradley's initial opening that day.

"…we believe it's the same killer as Jennifer Welt and Sarah Bondman, he would have buried them side-by-side."

Out of nowhere, this ominous deep raspy voice came on within the taping. "Help me!"

Kyle stopped the tape and eyed his mom. "That wasn't one of us, Mom."

"Did you have anything else taped on it perhaps and it came through?"

Kyle vehemently shook his head. "Nope. It was a brand new tape. But wait, that's not the best part. We thought that was the end of it…"

"But we had let the tape run when Kyle freaked on us," Shawn added.

"Listen, it continues." Kyle restarted the tape. Some static along with the rustling from their digging was heard before that same eerie voice popped up again.

"F…find cop." Then the tape came to an end.

"Find cop? I don't understand."

"Ma, *that* was the voice of old man Doorman. That wasn't the skeleton of a female victim. That was old man Doorman's spirit coming through, in the tape. Didn't you notice his stuttering?"

Susan leaned back against the chair, shaking her head. As wild and unbelievable as it sounded, Kyle was an intelligent boy and would never over embellish just for the sake of being unique, she thought. Yet, she needed more.

"Kyle, I don't understand. How's this possible?"

"You were there. You said I spoke those same words. Don't tell me you didn't feel anything weird. You said so yourself that *I* wasn't *me*." Kyle couldn't contain his excitement over this discovery. He kept shifting in his chair, looking back several times at his friends, then back to her. His friends high-fived each other.

Susan couldn't deny this fact—she had felt and heard something out of the norm while in the cave. From her recollection, Doorman's voice was raspy, always stuttering when excited to talk about something interesting or important to him. Yet, as the adult, she needed to pry some more. "And how can you say for sure it's Mr. Doorman?"

Bradley took out a newspaper clipping from his back pocket and sat beside Susan.

"We found an old article in a local trash magazine that had interviewed Doorman before he disappeared. Here." He smoothed out the article in front of her. Susan pulled it closer, folded and unfolded one corner of the paper before reading it out loud.

"Eugene Doorman appeared lucid and very articulate last night. Nothing compared to the so-called 'state of lunacy' he is characterized by. He clearly stated his vision of a cop as the suspect should be investigated. Captain McGuire reserved his comment to a few choice words. *"We should not feed Mr. Doorman's vampirism tendencies."* Thank you, Captain McGuire, for your police insight. The question remains: Who kidnapped and murdered these girls? Why is it such a ridiculous notion a cop may have committed these crimes? Haven't we in the past cooperated with different psychic mediums to help solve cases? Why not Eugene Doorman?"

Susan gently pushed the article back to Bradley. She bent her head, eyes closed, rubbing her temples. Richard's sinewy hand for solutions jumped in her thoughts and that longing for him hit harder than ever. The years together had planted some of his police instincts in her…but nothing registered at the moment. This was so out of the normal realm.

After several minutes of silence, she looked across at her son and his two best buddies. She struggled with how to structure her words without bashing their hopes.

"Kyle, this is a trash paper. You can't believe everything you read."

"No, but I sure believe what I hear. In the tape, if you put it together, he says 'help me find cop.'"

No denying this. Those words came out plain as day. Desperately trying to lift this drowning sensation of denial, she decided to open her mind to the possibility the boys may very well be onto something. Her train of thought changed.

"Let's say you're right, then the first thing we'll have to do is tell someone at the precinct about your find."

"Who? Mom, what if it's true, and it's a cop, who do we tell?" Kyle's blue eyes intensified in color. They were like a mood ring, only mood eyes that changed hues depending on his emotion. Susan couldn't help but reflect on how similar Kyle's features mirrored Richard's right now. From the way he cocked his head to the side, his intense eye contact when something of interest needed to be resolved...everything was so Richard. She thought hard and long for an answer. There was only one person she felt safe contacting.

"Stan. I'm calling Stan. If, by any chance, what you three discovered in the cave is Mr. Doorman's remains, they'll be able to confirm it, with all the forensic technology they have, and DNA testing."

"And then?" Kyle asked.

"One step at a time." Susan didn't have all the answers but one thing Richard had taught her was to organize your thoughts and start from the beginning. She got up, went to the phone, and poised her fingers to dial.

I need to get to the bottom of this madness.

Chapter Eleven

Several police cruisers, with their lights flashing, blocked the main entrance to Doorman's Creek. Officers had secured the area with yellow police tape surrounding the boys' Dinosaur Tree; two body bags were carried from the base of the tree to the back of the coroner's van. Several detectives and uniformed cops walked around, checking the grounds. Further in, more of those yellow 'No Trespassing' signs waved their tails by the slight breeze of the day. Susan, along with Kyle and Stan, emerged from the cave.

"Kyle, thanks to you and your friends, we're gonna have a couple of parents who can lay their daughters to rest at last," Stan said, placing an arm around Kyle.

"What about the skeleton inside the cave?" Kyle asked, abruptly.

Susan glanced at him. She noted the pale skin, the tired look around his eyes, and her own emotions tightened in her stomach. Anger over the unknown person who killed her husband kept her awake most nights, but the fear of anything happening to Kyle caused her to be cautious from now on. She had to be sure whatever information she shared would be to the right person. Kyle's feelings about an officer involved in the Doorman Creek murders stayed near in her thoughts.

"We're gonna send it to the lab for tests. Hopefully, we'll be able to identify the victim."

Stan lit a cigarette just before his features turned icy cold. His nostrils flared up like a bull about to charge.

Susan gave a courteous nod as Captain McGuire made his way toward them. She studied Stan's facial muscles tauten, his eyes narrowed almost to a squinting view. *What is it with you two?*

"I tell you it's old man Doorman." Kyle motioned with his hand back toward the cave, his tone adamant to that conviction.

Susan grasped his arm, giving it a sharp squeeze, hoping her son wouldn't continue.

"How can you be so sure, Kyle?" McGuire asked, stepping closer to him.

Worried Kyle might reveal his theory a cop is a murderer, Susan jumped in to answer before her son's adolescent mood kicked in and revealed more than she was willing to share.

"It's just that he disappeared, and we all know how much he loved the Creek, Kyle is just assuming he died here." She inhaled a deep, anxious breath, hoping her explanation would suffice McGuire.

Ignoring her, he continued to face the teen. "And, Kyle, how were you able to pinpoint which tree we'd find the dead girls in?"

McGuire wasn't giving up. He kept his vigilante stare on Kyle and this persistence irked her.

A frown creased his brow as Kyle glanced at his mom. He fidgeted with his hands before finally placing them in his front pockets.

"Kyle, go wait for me in the car, sweetie." She gave him a gentle nudge.

He didn't hesitate to leave.

"Captain…Mike," she said, once Kyle was out of range, "he's been through a lot, with his dad, and everything else. Can you question him later?" Susan tried the 'innocent' approach, anything to get McGuire off Kyle's back. He was smart, trying to pull Kyle in to talk about his intuition about old man Doorman, but she was a solid mountain that wouldn't budge where her son was concerned.

"Susan, we have to find out what else he knows. He might be in danger."

This had occurred to her, and the knot in her stomach tightened even further. Her head whirled with, '*Who is it?*' This only fortified her decision to be leery of what information she offered. At the moment, McGuire stood at the top of her list of suspects, but no reason to explain and comfort her why this strong intuition grabbed her emotions.

"If he's still having these dreams we discussed—"

"But he's not," Susan interrupted, trying to contain the quiver in her voice and sound as casual as possible.

"…there's a chance the killer will find out," McGuire mumbled, paying no attention to her obvious distress. Stan did, however, and came to stand beside her, one arm around her shoulders for comfort. She sighed, thankful for his interference.

"Captain, we don't have to name the kid. We can…"

Susan caught the sudden twitching in McGuire's eyes as he shifted his position to face his detective. "Stan, go make sure they're not mucking up the evidence in the cave."

She found him abrupt for no apparent reason. Stan grumbled something under his breath and left, grudgingly.

Just as quickly, McGuire turned on her; that same angry glint from a few minutes ago concentrating on her now.

"Susan, I asked you to tell me when Kyle was having more visions."

"He hasn't. This was just a coincidence."

"Okay, Susan, this is how you want to play it, fine. When you're ready to tell me everything, you know where to find me. This is *not* a coincidence. You're playing with fire and gambling with your son's life." McGuire stomped off toward the two body bags, leaving Susan wondering about the sudden interest in Kyle and his visions. She knew McGuire didn't believe in such things—Richard had told her on more than one occasion when a situation came about and they needed to call in a psychic to help with one of their cases. So why play the intimidating hand on her now? Why purposely place fear inside an already wounded person about her son's life in danger? *What game are you playing? What do you know?*

A sudden urge to call out to him and confide what the boys revealed to her in the tape tempted her. His genuine concern for Kyle sent mixed feelings that perhaps she may be mistaken about his involvement with Richard's murder and these Doorman killings. Then Richard's voice of reasoning she so often heard popped in her head, "Susan, in cases where I have more than one suspect guilty of a crime, I allow the game to play on with my guard up. Sooner or later, the actual suspect makes a mistake and I'll be there to catch them." *Thank you, sweetie.* She turned around and headed back to the car.

Kyle continued to look distressed; eyebrows set together like his dad used to do when he was puzzled by a case, and the biting of nails, another Richard trait he inherited.

Susan climbed into the car, securing the seatbelt.

"Why didn't you tell Captain McGuire the truth, Mom?" Kyle blurted.

"Just a feeling I have, that's all." She wasn't about to worry him with her female intuition...not yet.

Chapter Twelve

Kyle, Bradley, and Shawn sat cross-legged on Kyle's bedroom floor, newspaper clippings scattered all over the place.

"Let's go over everything we have," Kyle said, perusing all the info in front of them. The boys had gathered anything they could find to help them figure out this mystery.

They spent long hours scanning old newspaper clippings at the library, plus all the information Bradley had accumulated. Their piece of the puzzle was there, spread out like tiles ready to be placed in an orderly fashion. The elusive answer gnawed at Kyle, determined tonight would be the night they put their thinking caps on and solve it, even if it took all night.

Bradley adjusted his glasses and sat on his knees. Shawn shifted positions several times, staring at the pieces of their puzzle.

"Okay, we have the clippings of the girls identified ten years ago. Now, the ones with the other two girls that were found. That still leaves us with who was that we found in the cave?" Bradley glared at the articles, hunched forward in a doggy-style stance.

"I know it is or was…Doorman," Shawn said, his voice quivering near the end.

Kyle understood his friend's apprehension. The thought of someone being dead, yet able to communicate with you freaked him out, too. Their discussions centered lately over the tape recording and their reasoning, by the obvious stuttering of the voice, their ghost must be old man Doorman.

"I don't know. I feel it was, but those visions have confused me. I know whatever it made me see them wasn't going to hurt me." Kyle pushed back a lock of his auburn hair dangling in front of his eyes. The pictures and articles made no connection for him. The clue was in there somewhere, he *felt* it.

"So there, it's Doorman. If it was the killer, you'd feel threatened." Shawn snapped his fingers as though producing this hypothesis from out of a hat like a magician.

Kyle kept shaking his head. There was more to it and he aimed to find out what.

"Maybe. Bradley, where are the new clippings from the two missing girls from this year?"

Bradley shifted a few of the clippings out of the way and placed the ones Kyle wanted on top of the rest. "Here."

Kyle picked one of them up and read aloud, "Meagan Ways, 22, was last seen at the end of her shift at a local market by a co-worker near the downtown district last night.

Any information about this case will be kept confidential. Contact Detective Anderson."

Kyle felt the blood drain from his face. It took every ounce of power he had to keep his cool and not shed a tear at the mention of his dad.

"You okay, pal?" Bradley said, patting Kyle on the shoulder.

"Your dad was on this case?" Shawn looked as though he had just come out of a space shuttle, all disoriented and confused.

"He had worked on the Doorman murders, so he got this case because it was similar, I guess. Anyway, I knew about it. This was his line of work. Where's the other clip on the last girl?" Kyle wanted to change the 'dad' topic as quickly as possible before those tears dropped.

Bradley did some more shuffling and handed Kyle another clipping. This one had a picture of the recent victim gone missing. Kyle studied the picture for quite some time.

There was something about her. He kept staring at her image, focused on her face.

"I *know* her! Where do I know her from?" He put the clip down, got up, and paced the room. "I know I've seen her somewhere." He walked by his bedroom window and looked out. The nagging intuition he knew her got stronger while he glanced at the empty street outside. His eyes followed the pathway leading to his entrance below. That's when it hit him. "She was outside my house," Kyle exclaimed, nice and loud. He spun around and faced his friends. "When did she disappear?" he asked while tromping back to the center of the room.

Bradley grabbed the clipping from the floor and quickly scanned it. "Saturday, June twenty."

"Hey, that's the night we found our dead friend, Mr. Bones, isn't it?" Shawn added.

"She was outside, with Lewis that night, kissing."

"You don't think he did it?" Bradley asked Kyle with a '*get outta here*' look plastered on his face.

“Let’s put all the girls down. See what we have.” Kyle and Bradley rearranged the clippings in chronological order. “Okay, we have:

Barbara Cambridge, 16.

Delilah Coolidge, 17.

Jennifer Welt, 17

Sarah Bondman, 17

“Now there’s Meagan Ways, 22,” Shawn added, placing the clipping he had with the others.

“And Frances Harold, 24,” Kyle finished, placing the last clip to the puzzle.

The boys stood around, studying the pictures intensely. Kyle paced around, trying to figure things out in his head.

“What’s the connection?” Kyle asked, one hand tapping the top of his head. He backed up as though the distance might help him see things a bit more clearly. He careened around the clippings, ending back in his original spot.

“How do we know there *is* a connection?” Shawn said. “Could be a coincidence. Another murderer.”

“No, there’s always a connection in murders that have had a lull in time and resurface at a later point. Could be a copycat murderer, yes, but there are far too many similarities with the old cases and those of the girls missing now,” Bradley said, shaking his head.

“None of them even look the same, to say they looked like somebody this creep hated enough to kill,” Shawn said, scrutinizing the pictures, picking them up one by one, and then tossing them back down.

Kyle let out an agitated ‘*Shawn!*’ and stooped down to switch the pictures to face upwards.

Shawn mumbled ‘Sorry’ and took a step back.

"They all disappeared or were last seen at different locations," Bradley said, rearranging the pictures to their original order. "Mind you, these places are not far away from each other."

Kyle stopped and just stared at the photos again. He kept drifting from one photo clip to the other. Then something came to him and he snapped his fingers. "Their ages!" he called out.

"What about them?" Shawn asked, scratching his head.

Bradley stood up and looked at Kyle with a knowing grin.

"What? What am I missing?" Shawn asked, staring at his friends, totally lost.

Bradley ignored Shawn's outburst and turned to Kyle. "You think?"

"It's been ten years. Older now. Would go after older ones," Kyle said, almost analyzing the new turn of events to himself. He started his pacing, excited with this new revelation.

"What are you two talking about?" Shawn asked again, grabbing Kyle by his shoulders, forcing him to stop his unrelenting pacing and look at him.

Kyle shrugged him off and, in turn, grabbed Shawn by his shoulders, staring at him intensely. His heartbeat thumped away as he tried to find the words to make Shawn understand what the excitement was all about.

"Lewis was, ten years ago, around eighteen. His victims would have been closer to his age."

"Ten years later, they would still be closer to his age, more or less," Bradley said, picking up the information where Kyle left off.

Kyle let go of Shawn and turned to Bradley. "We've got to go tell my mom."

* * * *

Kyle's jaw muscles worked up a storm as he rambled on about the newest theory they came up with to his mom. The deep, tired lines around his eyes made him appear older than the teenager he was. Susan glanced over to Bradley and his wide-eyed stance, then to Shawn who, surprisingly, was listening attentively.

"I don't know, Kyle." Lewis, as a suspect, never crossed her mind. Susan still had a hard time coming up with a reason Captain McGuire remained so adamantly in her head as the possible suspect. His persistence to find out when Kyle had a vision should have eased her worries that he cared…but it didn't. This new development turned her investigation for a loop. *Lewis?*

"Mom, think about it. Lewis is the perfect age, then and now."

Susan kept shaking her head. "Captain McGuire was the officer in charge back then." For a flitting moment, she wished for an escape to a faraway sanctuary or even to a realm where time could be reversed and find herself home, beside Richard. *Maybe*…just maybe she may have been able to save his life. Shawn's abrupt tug on her arm snapped her out of that stupor.

"He probably covered up for him. What, turn in his own son?" Shawn said.

"Mom, you okay?"

Susan noticed the concern written on his face. She put a hand on her right temple and gently massaged the throbbing beat of the headache's drum. "You boys should be out, going to the movies, meeting girls, not locked upstairs investigating murders." Guilt swallowed her whole.

"Mom, we *need* to do this. Don't worry about us." Kyle offered a reassuring smile.

She managed a weak smile. "Shawn," she said, turning to face him, "I've thought of that, but Richard was working on the case with him. They had no leads. Except…"

Susan stopped midstream and went over to the refrigerator door. She removed a slip of paper from the bulletin board.

"I found these notes in your dad's agenda, along with another he had scribbled on and stuffed in his jacket. It mentions a club, Ecstatica, and two witnesses. Hold on…" She picked up the receiver and began to dial.

"Who you calling, mom?"

"I'm calling these witnesses to see if your father had questioned any of them around the time of his death."

Within seconds, Susan placed the receiver back on its hook.

"The first number is no longer in service. Let me try the other one." She looked over the number and started to dial once again.

"Yeah," answered a female, sounding annoyed.

"Hello. Can I speak with Nadine, please?"

"Yeah, it's me," came the abrupt answer.

"Hello. My name is Susan and I'm calling–"

"Listen, I don't want to buy or listen to anything. Besides, it's fucking eight at night. Don't you guys quit after five?"

"No…no, I'm not selling anything. I'd like to know if Detective Richard Anderson had questioned you several weeks ago, about a murder investigation from ten years ago?"

"You a cop?"

"No, I'm his wife."

"Nothing happened between us, lady. He's cute, but not my type. A pain in the butt, actually."

"My husband was killed," Susan spat in anger, "and I'm just trying to piece together what he might have been working on." A surge of anger at this woman's rudeness radiated but refrained from any comment.

There was a lull for a few seconds before the voice on the line spoke again. "I'm sorry. He…well, anyway, yeah, he came by, I'd say around then and I told him, like I told the other cop from years ago, that there was this guy who picked up the girl that got killed from this club I used to go to, Ecstatica. Didn't see his face."

"That's it?" Susan felt numb. Once again that club came to the forefront, but she took a satisfying gulp. She was on the right track.

"That's all. Then your hubby got up and left."

"I'm sorry for disturbing you. Thank you."

"No problem and…I'm sorry," Nadine said, then hung up.

Susan stared at the three curious boys across the room, then inhaled a deep breath and let it out in a slow sigh.

"Well, we now know he had or was investigating this club," Susan said, her mind wondering what her next step should be. She desperately tried to place herself in Richard's shoes, in a cop's frame of mind, to help her out.

"So, what do we do?" Kyle immediately said, causing Susan to see how alike their thinking was. She turned her focus to the two boys who were eyeing her closely.

"Boys, you two are going home."

"Mom, *please*, can they stay overnight?" Kyle scowled at her, his annoyed tone noted.

"No. I'll drop you two off at your homes. Kyle, you wait here. I'll be back."

"Where you going?"

Instinctively, Susan thought it best not to divulge any information to her son at that moment. The least he knew, the less worried he'd be.

Chapter Thirteen

"Susan, think of what you're saying! It's ludicrous," Stan said, walking away from her. She grabbed a hold of his arm and swung him around to face her.

"Stan, Kyle is right. Lewis would have been the perfect age, then *and* now. I didn't believe it at first, but it makes sense."

"It's all circumstantial evidence. You know that won't hold up in a court of law."

He loosened her grip and she followed him down the long hallway of his home, turning to the right, into his kitchen. Stan walked up to the butcher-top counter, reached over to the cupboard, and took out two mugs. "Coffee?"

"No, thanks. So, what, we wait till a new victim turns up missing?" she vehemently spat.

"That's not what I'm saying." He left her empty mug on the counter and poured himself a cup of coffee before settling down on the pine kitchen table set in the middle of the room. Susan sat opposite him.

"So, *help* me," she implored, her gut clenched tightly, despising having to beg for help. Imprisoned with only circumstantial evidence, Susan knew only too well the predicament Stan faced, but without his help, she didn't know where else to turn.

"I can't go after McGuire, or his son without proof," Stan stammered. "There's enough animosity between us as it is. I go after him and it'll look like I'm trying to pin anything on him as revenge for being such an asshole to me." He slammed his fist against the table, startling her. "The prick went and gave me desk duty…*me*…desk duty. I never roughed up that stupid chick. If I had, she would have been in worse shape than she was. And Richard was no goddamn help…" He stopped in midstream, turning to look at her. "Listen, I had suspicions about Lewis, told the captain, but it went nowhere then. After that, his attitude toward me changed, so you can see why I'm hesitant to go after his son without proof."

She was motionless for a split second until an idea formed. "Okay. Follow him. Go to this club and check it out for me." Susan completely ignored his last remark about Richard. She knew all about Stan's mood swings; Richard had mentioned the case about the hooker being beaten, and the charges laid against Stan. Richard never believed one hundred percent Stan did it but did agree with the psych evaluation. It was based on his recommendation Stan had six weeks of therapy sessions for anger management and eventually got desk duty temporarily. They found Stan innocent after an initial investigation discovered the hooker had a history of placing complaints against all cops who arrested her. Also, a material witness came forth and claimed to have been in a bar when the hooker picked a fight with another call girl hitting on her client.

"Fine. Let me see what I can do. In the meantime, stay out of trouble. Kyle too. Understood?"

"Scouts honor." She let out a small breath of relief, leaning back against the chair and accepting his offer for coffee now. "And thank you for confirming your suspicions about Lewis. Makes me feel we're on the right track."

Her gaze wandered to the paper spread out on the table. The heading: Teen Girl Still Missing And Presumed Dead!

There was no question in her mind now; they needed to find the killer before another innocent victim went missing. This vicious cold case circle had to come to a stop.

* * * *

"Kyle, I'm home." After a second or two, she called out his name again. A flashback to the night she discovered Richard's body in the kitchen hit her. Fearing the worst, she rushed in that direction. Kyle wasn't there. She glanced quickly at the living room before taking the steps two at a time to the first floor and then ran into his bedroom. His room was empty.

She frantically searched the entire house.

"Kyle, where are you?" Fear shot through her adrenaline-charged mind. Instead of Richard in a pool of blood, closed eyes brought up images of her son in that position but on a slab of concrete, out of her reach and protection. She opened her eyes, wiping away tears.

The sound of the back door slamming shut startled her. Careful not to make a sound, she picked up the vase from the hall console beside the kitchen entrance. Arms stretched above her head, back pressed against the wall, vase poised to smash over the figure coming out through the door, she waited. Her breathing came in heavy, gaze never faltering from the kitchen doorway, but her hands trembled as the footsteps neared.

Kyle, stunned, looked up at his mom as he stepped into the hallway.

"Kyle!" She backed away, placing the vase back on the console. "Where the hell were you? You scared the shit out of me."

"I saw Lewis and Mr. McGuire out in front of their home, arguing, so I snuck out to try and eavesdrop."

"Are you mad? I told you to stay put." The urge to have a smoke hit her hard. She never smoked…but this was as good a time as any, she figured. Her rattled nerves couldn't take much more. It took every bit of energy not to shake some sense into her son. The blood…Richard on the floor… all these images she hoped were gone came back with a vengeance, churning her insides.

"They didn't see me. Anyways, Mr. McGuire was yelling at Lewis for not taking his pills again. Lewis told him to…well…to f-off then took off in his car. The captain ran down the driveway, yelling at him to stay away from that club."

"Ecstatica. Okay. Stay put. And I *mean* stay put. I'm going to this club. If I'm not back in a couple of hours call Stan at the station. Tell him where I've gone."

"You can't go alone. Please, mom. Let me come."

"No." One short response with such conviction and finality, Kyle didn't argue.

"Mom, be careful, please."

The worried tone broke her heart. She approached and gave him a reassuring hug. "Don't worry, sweetie. I'm not going to do anything stupid like you might." She smiled and left before he could convince her to stay.

* * * *

Susan parked the car across the street and eyed the people walking in front of the club. She spotted Lewis, dressed in black jeans and a black shirt, talking to some people. His attention turned to a pretty brunette, hugging and kissing her before they entered the club.

Getting out of the car, Susan was surprised to see Stan in the distance, heading toward the club. *Oh, Kyle, I told you to wait before calling Stan.*

Hiding amidst a group of club dwellers, Susan entered the club undetected by Stan or Lewis. Several people were dancing up a storm as she carefully made her way to a secluded table at the back. Lewis was heading to the dance floor with the girl while another young pretty female, obviously intoxicated by the way she was carrying herself, tried to strike up a conversation with Stan at the bar.

When she looked back at the dance floor, Lewis was gone. Frantically, she scanned the club and eased up when she spotted him taking a seat with his date. He leaned over, and whispered something in her ear before heading toward the bar.

Susan stayed in the corner, obscured from both of them. Stan appeared to be flirting with that bimbo at the bar.

What the hell are you doing, Stan?

Lewis had reached the bar by now and slapped the detective on the back. The men exchanged handshakes as Susan made her way closer to eavesdrop, close enough to hear over the ruckus of the music.

"Hey, Detective, fancy meeting you here."

Susan stood in the background, behind one of the decorative free-standing tall and wide plants, listening. Between the long, silky fake leaves obscuring her presence from them, she concentrated on their lips, trying to pick up words she couldn't hear properly.

"Hey, Lewis, how are you?"

"Could be better."

"Your dad's still on your ass?"

"Can't seem to shake him off. You on duty?"

Stan showcased a sly grin. "No, just relaxing." He took a quick glance over at Lewis' table. "Nice looking girl."

"Her name's Brigitte, a friend from my therapy group. She's been helping me deal with some stuff."

"Well, good for you. You haven't experienced any more memory losses or blackouts? Maybe nausea, headaches–"

"No, sir. It happened only once, and that's because I got piss drunk with some friends years ago. Anyway, it was nice seeing you. Better head back."

Waiting until Lewis was back at his table, Susan made her way to Stan, making sure she had her back toward Lewis' table. The young thing drooling over Stan earlier now had her head resting on the bar.

Stan's brows furrowed as soon as he spotted her. "Susan, what are you doing here?" he said, a flash of surprise immediately replaced by a sneer.

"I can ask you the same question."

"I'm the cop, remember? I thought I told you to stay out of this."

"Kyle overheard McGuire and Lewis arguing about his medication and warned him to stay out of this place, so I decided to come here and spy on him myself."

"I want you to go home. I'm looking into this. If anything comes up, I'll give you a shout."

Ignoring him, she peeked over her shoulder at Lewis and his date.

"Go home, Susan, I mean it." He gently held her arm and escorted her out of the club.

Susan thought better than to resist in case Lewis caught the bar commotion. She obediently followed Stan toward the exit, glancing one more time behind. Lewis was laughing, holding the young woman's hand.

Outside, they continued walking toward her car. "Your *son* doesn't need to be an orphan. Stop playing the role of a cop. I said if there's anything new, I'll let you know."

"Stan, he saw you. You spoke to him, for God's sake. You think he's going to make a move now?" Susan was beyond furious. She couldn't understand how Stan could follow Lewis now that he was spotted. Unsure what to do, she absentmindedly began to walk back toward the club when Stan grabbed her arm.

"Susan, please, just get in the car and go home. I know what I'm doing. Can you please trust me? I need to merge some sort of connection with Lewis, on his turf."

Staring at him for a few seconds, trying to calm jittery nerves and hide the shakiness in her voice, she reluctantly got in the car. She rolled down her window.

"The McGuires have something to do with this case, Stan, and I want to know how it involves Richard's death."

"All right, I promise I'll get back to you. You don't think *I* want to find out who killed Richard? You asked me to follow up on this club and that's what I'm doing. Please, just go home and let me do what I do best."

She regretted the distrustful tone toward the man helping her out. Realizing he was doing the best he could on his own time as well, she backed off and started the car.

She waved to him while driving off, watching him enter the club through her rear-view mirror.

A couple of blocks later, a deep impulse to turn around took hold. She pulled the car to the side. This intuition was strong, stronger than it ever was. "No, there's something that's not kosher here."

That gut feeling shook her into action. Making sure there was no oncoming traffic, she made a U-turn and headed back to the club. Married to a detective for so many years gave her the sense to park farther away from the club, close enough to eye the front entrance but far enough not to be seen.

Several patrons of the club began to exit about an hour or so later, but no sign of Stan or Lewis. *God, I hope I didn't miss them.* Her eyes felt heavy from lack of sleep, so she leaned her head back against the headrest for a few seconds.

* * * *

The dream was vivid. The pull to find out what was happening kept its insistent and inviting aura.

"Where we going, Kyle?"

Kyle motioned with his hands for her to follow him. They passed their driveway…in the next instant, they stood somewhere in Doorman's Creek.

"Kyle, where are you?" Susan looked all around. The faint crunching sound of footsteps somewhere behind startled her. Nothing out of the ordinary was visible. But as she slowly turned her head, that same Dr. Doom character

was now clearly visible by the entrance of the cave. A sharp female's voice cried out in the night, from within the cave. Dr. Doom disappeared and Susan rushed inside the opening. Kyle stood no more than a few feet ahead, his back turned toward her.

"Kyle, you okay?"

In slow motion, Kyle turned to face her, but Susan was now on a dirt road. A female in her mid-twenties was checking the inside of her hood. The headlights of another car blinded Susan for a second. A car door closed. Someone approached the young girl.

"Everything okay, Miss?"

"I think I did something to the engine. My parents are going to kill me."

"Here. Let me give you a lift to the gas station. You don't want to be here by yourself in the middle of nowhere."

"Well, I don't know..."

"Don't worry. I'm a cop."

He flashed what appeared to be a badge.

The dream suddenly changed; the girl was now on her knees, arms extended in front trying to protect herself.

"Please, I don't want to die. Leave me alone. Please. Noo!!!"

With his back turned, he hit the girl with the butt of his pistol. She fell hard on the ground, half unconscious. He scooped her up and carried her to a nearby tree.

She groaned softly as he discarded her with a heavy thud on the ground.

Leaning forward, both hands wrapped around her neck, choking her. In her weakened state, she was no match for him as she struggled to get free. With each fighting effort, he whacked her over the head until she finally passed out.

"Stop. Leave her alone!" Susan cried.

His back straightened, shoulders rolled once as he turned to face her.

Kyle woke up from his nightmare. *"MOM!"*

Chapter Fourteen

Susan yawned and stretched. Glancing at the radio clock in the car, more than half an hour had passed since she closed her eyes. *Shit.* Just as she began to think she may have missed them, out walked Stan with a different girl than the one at the bar, by his side.

"What the hell you doing, Stan? Where's Lewis? Shit, I must've missed him." Disappointed to have wasted all this time for nothing, she started the car. At the last second, she decided to follow Stan for a bit in case the girl was undercover with him, following Lewis somewhere.

* * * *

Kyle frantically dressed fast to get help. He still couldn't get over his vivid dream and who popped up as the killer.

He locked the door, jumped over the bushes, and ran straight toward McGuire's house.

"Please be home. Please be home," he kept saying, banging away at the front door like a madman.

Hearing a car approaching, Kyle turned around. The headlights blinded him for a second. He squinted to see who it was and spotted Lewis walking toward him.

* * * *

Susan followed Stan, making sure the taillights were off, keeping a distance not to be spotted. It surprised her how much she had learned from Richard over the years without realizing it. He would have been proud.

She parked far enough not to be seen when Stan came to a halt around a secluded road right outside Doorman's Creek. Stan leaned forward and kissed the girl.

"What the hell am I doing? I feel like a Peeping Tom, for Christ's sake." Feeling physically tired and emotionally drained, she wanted to get back home to Kyle, snuggle in her bed and revitalize herself for another round of 'find and seek' the next day. She gave one more glance toward Stan's parked vehicle before starting the car.

Suddenly, the girl flared her arms in the air. Susan saw Stan raise his hand and strike her.

"Oh my God!"

Stan came out, walked to the trunk, and opened it. A few seconds later, he walked around to the passenger side. Susan clearly saw him holding a black cape.

Before opening the door, Stan put on the cape, then dragged the unconscious girl out, tossing her over his shoulder.

"Oh my God, not you Stan." There was never a reason to suspect him from all people. He was there for her when her life tore apart, helping to piece this thing together. *Idiot! You played right into his hands.*

Numb, unsure what to do, she quietly closed her car door to follow him into the forest. Remembering the flashlight, she carefully opened the door again, trying her best not to make any noise. Retrieving the flashlight from the glove compartment, she left the door open this time.

"Great, Susan, protect yourself with a flashlight. Light him to death," she whispered, trying desperately to control the feeling edging up in her to hyperventilate. She chewed the inside of her mouth as she started out.

Susan couldn't see Stan but heard his heavy footing trampling through the twigs and the random moans of the girl.

Then nothing.

Panicking, she looked all around until a faint cry caught her ears.

She's still alive.

Susan upped her pace toward the sound, then stopped.

"No, please!" The girl's plea echoed in the quiet night.

"Shut up, *bitch*!"

"*Please...*"

"I told you to shut the fuck up!"

Another slap resonated amidst the poor girl's frantic pleas. She made a move forward but quickly stopped when she stepped on a twig, its snapping cutting into the other sounds. No more slaps now, but fast walking.

Where are you?

Desperately trying to hear where the footsteps were coming from, looking all around, when out of nowhere a punch slammed into her face.

* * * *

Dazed, Susan slowly opened her eyes. Her jaw hurt but moving it in circles, she knew it wasn't broken. The girl from the car lay right beside her, drenched in blood. Susan focused on the surroundings to determine where they were. The familiarity hit fast. They were in Kyle's cave. Then she spotted Stan, pacing back and forth, his gun firmly gripped. The cape was discarded nearby.

"You couldn't let well enough alone. You had to stick your nose into my affairs. Well now, you can witness all my fetishes up close."

"Stan, please."

"Oh, no 'Stan please, no, please don't hurt me'. Well, fuck you and fuck all bitches." His words cut through her like shears slicing away at a shrub. This side of Stan was new to her. She had witnessed one or two random outbursts in the past, but never anything of this magnitude. Richard had simply joked Stan's abrupt mood swings were because of a lack of sex. Everyone would laugh, Stan included.

He stepped forward and kicked the unconscious girl hard on her side.

"Leave her alone," Susan yelled, appalled at the random act. The nauseating dankness of the cave multiplied with the view of the defenseless girl lying still bit into her, hard. Their predicament didn't look good for either of them, especially when Stan looked like a bomb about to detonate.

Stan snickered, leaned forward, and grabbed Susan by the neck. "Don't you fucking tell me what to do. Your husband did, the captain did, the bloody police psych did…"

Susan looked into his cold, pitiless, vacant eyes and all she saw was a madman staring back. His grip around her neck tightened, and she fought to pry his hands loose.

"Stan…you're…cho…king…me."

As if slapped in the face, Stan released his grip and pushed her back. "I told you to go home at Ecstatica. I liked you, but you had to snoop, just like your husband."

"What do you mean?" Everything was drowned out by the blood rushing to her ears once his meaning became clear. "*You* killed Richard? You bastard!" Furious, her foot reached out to kick him while on the floor. She missed, and he came in quick, whacking her on the side of her face, knocking her sideways.

"Yes, I killed Richard. It's because of *your* husband they gave me desk duty. If he hadn't suggested an evaluation, I'd still have all my duties intact. But no, he said I was having mood swings. So, I got desk duty till I finished my fucking therapy. They reduced me to nothing more than a secretary." Stan kicked away at the dirt. "Anyway, he started digging up the Creek murders because of your psycho son, and eventually, he would have figured it out. So, yeah, I killed him. Went over to your lovely home, noticed the captain was in there, waited till he left, then I showed up. Had a coffee, and then I shot him, point-blank." Paper-thin lips highlighted a smug and arrogant grin.

A mental image assaulted her thoughts—Richard lying in a pool of blood. Susan grimaced, head shaking, desperate to erase that ugly scenario.

"Why did you kill all those girls, you sick bastard?"

"Sick? Nah. They had it coming to them. And if you're waiting to analyze me, don't. I had a perfect childhood. Mom doted on me. Dad, not so much. Hated my relationship with her up to the day he died. Then she died, leaving me his debt to inherit." His eyes changed, squinted in deep thought before his gaze snapped back to her.

"So stop analyzing me. I just love to kick some girl ass, if you know what I mean. They pretend as though they're going to put out and then, at the last moment, become teasers. They had it coming, like Miss All Innocent here. Didn't flinch once touching my crotch at the club, but once it got all private in the car…whore scum, just like the rest of them."

She watched as an unrelenting, crazed glint settled in his eyes again for a few minutes, as though thinking back to some of his conquests. Susan groaned, repulsed, sending Stan's stares once more toward her. A creeping dread of doom took over as she desperately tried to figure a way out of this situation.

"What's the matter, Susan, scared?" He swung his leg toward her, stopping within inches of her nose, leg extended in a karate stance. Susan shut her eyes, waiting for the impact that never came.

A madman's laughter echoed within the cave as Stan took a couple of steps back.

"I had plans for you, *Mrs.* Anderson, grand plans to erase Richard from your mind and replace him with my warm body at night in your bed." Susan shuddered. "Guess I'll have to look elsewhere now."

From the corner of her eye, she spotted movement from the cave's entrance. A thankful breath was inhaled when she noticed Captain McGuire quietly making his way toward them. He motioned with a finger to his lips for her to be quiet. She needed to distract Stan to give McGuire time to get to him with no detection.

"What are you going to do now?" she asked, her eyes focused entirely on Stan, careful not to give away the captain's whereabouts.

"Well, after I have some fun with this bitch, I'll jump on to you. By the time they find you, well, I guess I'll be the investigating officer of this case. My desk duty period is almost over. I've been a good boy." He laughed.

"I don't think so, Stan." McGuire appeared a few feet away, his gun drawn and aimed at Stan.

Without a twitch, Stan turned and faced him. Susan inched closer to the unconscious girl. Her eyes were almost completely closed and swelled, lips looking as though she took an overdose of silicone shots. Susan could see her stomach rise and fall with each forced breath, offering hope there was time to save this young girl.

"Well, Captain, nice of you to join the party." Stan's voice was mocking, with no hint of fear, whatsoever. He stepped in front, gun aimed at Susan, as he made his way over to her, always keeping McGuire in his eye-view. Bending down, Stan jerked her roughly by the hair. Susan yelled as Stan continued his firm yanking and pulling, dragging her several feet forward, losing her balance a few times.

"I see we're at a standoff. You shoot me, I shoot Susan. Boo hoo."

She watched as Stan and McGuire locked stares, each waiting for the other's first move. Stan's madman chant, '*Come on, shoot if you dare*' beckoned to the captain to shoot while the nozzle placed by her temple sent uncontrollable trembles throughout her body.

"Put the gun down, Stan, and I promise to get you some help," McGuire called out, both hands firmly gripping his gun. Specks of sweat formed on his forehead.

"Sorry, Chief. No can do. Don't forget, I still have the title detective, so I know how it works. Tell you what, you put your gun down and I'll promise to kill you quickly." Stan's laughter echoed like a sickly character from a bad horror flick.

McGuire dared to take a few steps forward.

"Uh uh. One more step and I'll shoot her." Stan's fingers curled tighter in Susan's hair. She swallowed a painful whimper, desperate to keep her wits about her. She tried to push away, but he only tightened his grip, yanking her head back harshly.

McGuire stopped his approach. "Listen, Stan, surrender now and I promise to get you the help you need. You're not well."

"The help I need?"

Panic heightened. The tone in Stan's voice depicted one who was about to lose his patience. A part of her dictated to stay calm; the more on edge she was, the more likely she'd miss an opportunity to escape. Focus, be alert, but her body shivered, choking down the lump in her throat to hurl. She eyed McGuire, and a guilty feeling now wedged between her fear. All the signs had pointed toward him as the wrongdoer. There was no way she, or anyone else, could have suspected Stan.

Had Richard?

Drained by the guilt and physical hurt, she sank to the floor, hoping her dead weight would be too much for Stan's one-handed grip. No dice. A throbbing on the side of her head slowly found its way to her eyes, tearing them up. She wiped the obstructing flow, clearing her eyesight. When she looked up again, her heart churned its beat faster when she spotted Kyle running past McGuire toward her.

"Mom!"

Susan saw the terror etched in Kyle's eyes. They were opened wide, flittering back and forth to Susan, the girl lying beside her, then back to his mother. At this point, it crossed Susan's mind Kyle may have not even realized Stan was standing there with the gun pointed at McGuire.

"Kyle, no…" Susan yelled.

Stan took this opportunity, while McGuire's attention focused on trying to reach Kyle and hold him back, to shoot. He shot Kyle in the leg.

As the captain made a move to jump Stan, he was shot, instantly dropping to the floor. Stan released his grip on Susan, letting her run to Kyle's aid.

"Well this has turned into a fuckin' party," Stan said, pacing a few feet up and down, keeping a watchful eye on everyone. He paused, a twisted smirk forming, then turned to face Captain McGuire sprawled on the floor. "Actually, it's perfect. Psycho captain tries to cover up the sick kid and kills witnesses. I love it." Stan hummed a happy chant, "Perfect, perfect, couldn't be better", like a madman without his straitjacket.

"Kyle, sweetheart, you okay?" Susan frantically searched how much blood gushed from his wound. She leaned over and gently removed the injured girl's bandana, and wrapped it around his leg for pressure to stop the bleeding. Blood splattered and meshed all over her hands while she caressed Kyle's face. His eyes were weak, signifying substantial blood loss.

"Don't bother, Susan. The kid's dead, just like you." Stan's venomous tone sparked an elevated fear that time was running out for them.

As she was about to say something, Kyle started to tremble. His whole body convulsed.

"Kyle!" *I'm losing him.*

With no other movement or opening of the eyes, Kyle's voice amplified, "No!" in that same deep, strange voice Susan had witnessed not too long ago.

Stan waved his hands about as though shooing flies. Unexpectedly, his body was hurled across the room by an unseen force, landing him with a thunderous jolt against one of the inner walls. He slumped down, unconscious, gun still in his grasp. Susan shook a pale-faced Kyle by the shoulders, certain this unknown entity had possessed her son again.

"Kyle! Kyle!"

He opened his eyes, blinking several times. "Mom?"

"Kyle, can you walk?" Susan said, demanding his attention while her stomach muscles punched a mean, sharp pain all the way to her back. At this point, the pain pummelling the back of her head and temples with the one jolting up her back came in equal on the 'aggravated soreness' chart.

He tried getting up on his own, but the pain from the gunshot obviously overwhelmed him. Susan helped him to his feet, supporting him with her arms, and together, hastened to the exit. She gave one quick glance toward Stan, making sure his lightbulbs were still in dreamland.

They limped a short distance until Susan set Kyle by a tree not too far from the entrance of the cave. "Kyle, I want you to hide here. Don't make a sound. No matter what! I'm going back to get Captain McGuire and the girl." She tasted blood on her tongue. Touching it with her index finger, she felt a cut on the side of her tongue.

"Mom, no, please. The police are on their way." Susan sensed his fear, validating her own at what she still needed to accomplish before Stan came to.

She locked fingers with him, offering a small smile. "I'll be fine, Kyle. Stay here."

Inhaling a long, steady breath, she walked back into the cave. Once inside, a frigid chill sent shivers all over her body.

An intuition the cold had more to do with whatever possessed this cave than the climate outside.

With the thought pushed out of her head, she mustered as much energy as possible and forged on.

Reaching her destination, she bent down and checked on McGuire; bleeding from his shoulder and still out cold. She removed his belt, wrapping it around his upper arm tightly. A faint moan caught her attention. Looking across the enclosure, she noticed the young woman stirring, her feet twitching. Susan left McGuire's side to help the injured girl.

"Can you hear me?" Susan said, leaning down. A weak nod came in reply. "Try to get up. Help me or else he'll come to and we're through." Wrapping her arm around the girl's shoulder, Susan steadied her to her feet. A few escaped moans of agony grimaced across the girl's face as she wobbled out with Susan's help.

Susan's anxiety shot through the roof once they exited the cave. *Need to go back for McGuire.* Kyle reached up and helped his mom place the girl on the ground beside him.

"Kyle, keep an eye out for her till the police get here. I'm going back for McGuire." Giving Kyle a glance of reassurance, she inhaled a deep, calming breath and re-entered the cave.

Instinctively, she glanced at Stan… *Good. Still out cold.* She knelt and tried to lift McGuire. His unconscious state made his dead weight impossible to lift him. She tried to turn him around by his feet to drag him out when, suddenly, she was yanked backward by the hair. She screamed at the sudden assault and let go of McGuire's legs.

"Aw, Susan, you've been a bad girl." Stan tossed her to the floor. She backed up against the wall, her hands scraping rocks.

"Stan, you can still get help." Her mind feverishly worked overtime to get him talking, stalling in the hopes the cops would get there in time.

"Thanks for the concern, but I don't think I'll take your advice. I suspect, in the state Kyle and our little bitch are in, they're probably right outside. Can't get too far. Your son punches a powerful apparition, Susan. Guess Doorman is still pissed at me for killing him."

"Why? Why would you kill him?"

"Didn't know the old bugger camped out here. He witnessed one of my moments with two of my girls. Couldn't have that. So, I killed the old fart, right here." Stan motioned with his hands how he struck Doorman. "Bang, right across the head with my shovel several times, and down he came. Not a whimper. Buried him half dead. Wonder how long he lasted, the old fool…buried *alive*."

"You're a sick prick," Susan spat, catching Stan's repulsive grin as he laughed.

"Heard it all before. Save your breath."

"Why the cape?"

"I tried to pin it on Doorman, but your husband wasn't biting. Not enough evidence, he said. So I decided to pin it on Lewis then. He frequented Ecstatica, he was there the nights I picked up the girls from the club and he was on and off on his antidepressant drugs from way back then. But McGuire chose to ignore these clues pointing at his kid. Plan C never came around to throw more suspicion on Lewis because of your meddling. So, my dilemma is to put the rap on McGuire. I came around just after he went crazy and killed you, Kyle, and our little slut. I had no choice but to shoot him. Self-defense."

Susan watched his impassive features, the slight twitching of the lips as he recounted his plan of escape to innocence. The more she studied him, the more she realized she never really knew Stan. Something dark lurked in the recesses of his mind she just couldn't apprehend.

"You'll never get away with it. Kyle's on his way to the police right now."

"Susan, Kyle is right outside, bleeding to death. I might be a sick prick like you put it, but I'm not a stupid prick." He reached down, grabbed her by one arm, and tugged her toward the exit. She wiggled to free herself but soon gave up after a few swift kicks to the gut.

Susan stumbled forward as he lugged her out of the cave's entrance. She eyeballed the area where she left Kyle and the girl. They were safely out of view. As long as Kyle remained quiet and Stan didn't venture to find him, they were secure for the moment. *Where are the police?*

"Oh, Kyle, I have your mommy. Come out, come out, wherever you are." Stan's sing-song tone grated on her nerves.

"He's not here, I tell you. He went to get the police."

Stan ignored the outburst and continued with his childish, playful voice. "Kyle, I'll count up to ten, then I'll shoot your mother. Ten…nine…"

"Don't listen, Kyle."

"Not a smart move, Susan. Eight, seven, six, five…come on, Kyle."

"Kyle, don't listen."

With one hand locked firmly around her hair, Stan backhanded her across the face with the butt end of the gun. She cried out in pain just as Kyle crawled/limped his way from behind the tree.

"There's our boy. And I suspect our princess is nearby."

Letting go of her hair, Stan walked up to the tree and looked behind where Kyle had appeared from. Susan dragged herself up to Kyle, shielding him in her arms.

"Yep, there's our sleeping beauty."

"Stan, please, leave us alone. You have ample time to run and hide before anyone finds us."

"Oh, it'll be quite some time before anyone finds you, that's for sure," he said, leaning closer to the unconscious girl.

Susan's heart squeezed tight as the implication of what Stan just said hit her.

"Surprised she's still alive. She's a tough one," he said, walking back toward Susan and Kyle. "No matter, she'll be gone in just a few minutes, anyway. Let her enjoy her dream-state for the time being."

He ran a finger across the barrel of his gun while his lips curled into a grin.

"You decide, Susan. Kyle?" He aimed the gun at her son. "Or Sleeping Beauty?" He then positioned his revolver toward the tree where the girl lay.

She felt suffocated between fear and anger at him, unable to concentrate and come up with a plan of escape.

He cleared his throat, snapping his fingers. "Susan! I need an answer."

His command resonated in her head.

* * * *

Police cars were parked by the Creek, just a few hundred yards from the cave's location. Lewis stepped out from one of the cars, followed by Phil, Shawn, and Bradley.

"Boys, where exactly is this cave of yours?" Phil asked.

Shawn pointed straight ahead.

All four, followed closely by officers with their weapons drawn, made their way through Doorman's Creek.

* * * *

"Too hard of a decision, Susan?" Stan laughed.

She remained speechless while his lunatic laughter edged itself further into her exhausted body.

"As much as I'd like to end this inside the cave because it's so symbolic for me, I'm not taking a chance on our friend Doorman coming through Kyle again. He throws a nasty punch."

He cracked his head from side to side before aiming the gun back at them. "I'm sorry it has to end like this. I had other plans for you, Susan."

Her pulse beat at her temples, but she maintained a tight hold on Kyle, drawing him closer. Her son squeezed her arm.

"What's the matter, Susan? You don't look excited?"

"What?" His question caught her off guard, its clarity unclear.

"Well…" He giggled. "…I'm going to reunite you with Richard. Thought you'd love a family reunion."

"You *bastard*!" she cried out, about to lunge at Stan. Kyle placed his upper body against her and stopped her.

At that moment, Susan heard a gunshot, and time seemed to slow down; Stan's eyes opened wide, a painful and shocked look taking over his features. A low gurgling sound, like a suppressed cough, along with traces of saliva that dribbled down the corner of his mouth.

As Stan slowly turned his head toward the direction of the gunshot, Susan leaned to her side for a better view.

By the entrance of the cave stood McGuire, his gun still smoking from the shot.

However, Susan felt recognition in the Captain's face, one not belonging to him at all.

"Enough k-k-killing." McGuire's mouth spoke those words, but it was old man Doorman's voice reaching across the distance to Susan.

McGuire lifted the gun and shot Stan again. With a stunned look plastered on his face, Stan fell hard to the ground, air rushing out of his body in heavy gasps. His body trembled for a few minutes before it seized its last spasms.

McGuire's body shook violently, almost at the exact moment Stan took his final breath.

Lewis, Phil, Shawn, and Bradley came running through the forest at that moment.

"Dad!" Lewis cried out, witnessing his father's epileptic tumble. He ran past several officers already headed toward their captain's aid.

Within seconds, police officers overran Doorman's Creek. Susan spotted Phil running toward them.

"Susan, Kyle, you guys all right?" Phil knelt, examining the severity of Kyle's wound. Every slight touch brought a grimace and an escaped moan from the teen, balling up his hands into fists.

The sirens of ambulances nearby warmed Susan's insides, knowing Kyle will shortly be on his way to the hospital.

Shawn and Bradley darted to Kyle and his demeanor suddenly changed, one to extreme 'glad to see you guys… *alive*'.

"There's a girl badly hurt at the base of the tree there, Phil," Susan said, pointing toward the tree she had left Stan's intended victim, her voice a frail whisper.

After assessing Kyle's wounds, Phil proceeded toward the girl. He stood up and whistled to the ambulance attendants approaching their area. "Over here. We have three injured, one with a gunshot wound to the leg, the other to the shoulder, and a female badly beaten."

Susan limped her way to the young girl, knelt, and held her hand.

"Thank you," the girl mumbled, her eyes swelled from the beating Stan gave her. Her lips were bruised and traces of dried blood clung to the edges.

"You're safe now. Don't try to speak," Susan said, stroking the girl's hair. Her first instinct…to cry, cry for this young girl and what occurred, cry for her son, for the other murdered girls by Stan's twisted mind…and for her husband. She took in a few quick breaths and turned her focus on Phil. "How did you find us?"

"Lewis called me at the station and told me what Kyle had told him and the captain. About his dream, seeing Stan."

"He dreamt of Stan?" Susan looked over at Kyle while a medic worked on him before placing him on a stretcher. Shawn and Bradley stood by Kyle's side, their faces slowly getting their natural color compared to the ashen looks they both displayed after witnessing the bloody scene before them.

"You've got an amazing kid there, Susan. If the captain wouldn't have also called in, I just may have thought Lewis was drunk. I mean, dreams, Stan a killer?" He shook his head. "And the tests came in today. Our skeleton friend is, indeed, like Kyle said, Eugene Doorman."

Phil helped Susan walk up to Kyle as they placed him on the gurney. Shawn and Bradley were high-fiving their friend.

"You're the man, Kyle. You're the man," Shawn said.

"Maybe we should get involved in something a little bit less dangerous next time. No?" Bradley said, smiling.

Kyle returned the smile.

Shawn snickered. "Some detective you'll make."

Bradley punched him in the arm, and all three laughed.

Watching the boys in their usual playful mode brought a lump to her throat. The excruciating fear suffered during these long, stressful weeks finally had ended. She watched solemnly as an officer zipped the bag and enclosed Stan's body. An involuntary shiver passed through her, releasing finally the despair that had consumed her for so long.

Holding Kyle's hand, Susan limped beside him as they wheeled him to the ambulance.

"Everything's all right now, sweetie."

"There's one thing we have to do, mom."

Susan leaned forward and listened to Kyle's request.

* * * *

A week later, Susan still sported a limb as she placed a rose on the gravesite by the entrance of the cave. The constant kicks by Stan to the abdomen resulted in a few broken ribs. McGuire supported her by gently holding on to her arm, while a sling hung across his chest for his own sustained injury. All four boys walked in unison behind the two adults, their black attire out of place for these surroundings yet so meaningful for the occasion they gathered today.

"Thank you for our lives. I hope you've found peace at last," Susan said, just as the chirping of birds began in unison and the sun's rays touched her cheeks. She could feel the release of the misery that occupied Doorman's Creek for such a long time. The whole ambiance had changed. Looking up, the bright blue skies gleamed through the forest's canopy of trees. The creek shadowed a faint tracing of the rainbow on the horizon from yesterday's downpour. The reflecting colors danced a twinkling soft ripple across the manmade Creek, erasing any dark hues within the once mysterious borders of Doorman's Creek.

Kyle, holding a black cape, hobbled on his crutches, with the help of Shawn and Bradley, to the gravesite.

"It belongs to him. He loved wearing it," Kyle said, placing it on the lonely grave.

McGuire turned to Susan. "It's funny how things come about. We originally believed Doorman was involved with the girls' disappearances and deaths all because of those markings on their necks. The lab results showed it came from some sort of handmade instrument and not actual bite marks, but without locating Doorman, not knowing exactly where he was from one moment to the next, we couldn't move on. By the time Eugene was spotted, he'd up and disappeared again.

"Then I began suspecting Stan after Lewis had mentioned to me he had seen him at this club. But I couldn't get any dirt on him. The son of a bitch had a mean streak in him. Richard had witnessed it a few times when they were out on an investigation. Stan covered it up pretty good with the shrinks. Couldn't fool me, though. I never mentioned my suspicions to Richard since they were partners at the time and I really didn't have any proof other than a gut feeling. But I did tell him everything the day he was killed. I knew Stan tried to draw suspicion onto Lewis. In all honesty, Susan, not once did I suspect my son. My experience dictated that Stan was involved, but without proof, I just couldn't pursue it other than to keep a close eye on him.

"Then Stan became the model cop and after a while, with no evidence to support my theory, I had no choice but to drop it. I had almost forgotten the emotions surrounding my intuition about Stan until these new disappearances crept up again.

"If I didn't experience it, I'd never have believed it. Eugene Doorman, after all these years, helped put an end to the Creek murders." McGuire stood with Lewis by his side, shaking his head in disbelief and wonderment, while Susan continued to look at the grave.

"And to his own, Mike. This is a fitting tribute to him. He loved this Creek."

She gave a quick look toward the cave's entrance, remembering the foreboding person standing there in all of her dreams. "He tried to communicate with me, Mike, through my dreams but I never put it together." The dark shadow, now apparently clearer to her, tried to indicate Doorman's black cape; the cave desperately showing where his remains lay.

"Susan, don't agonize over your dream. He managed, a bit through you and Kyle, to finally let his story be told. But also helped us locate those other missing girls and offer some peace to their parents. Locating his cape and that bite-mark handmade instrument Stan came up with to throw suspicion on Doorman…I'm just glad all the answers finally came through."

A mysterious engraver had etched the perfect words to symbolize Eugene's life. Susan suspected McGuire was the one who suggested the words on Eugene's headstone that read:

Eugene Doorman
Our town hero
And keeper of Doorman's Creek

The birds flew, crickets beat their melody into the air, a peaceful and serene scene replaced the once ominous and dank haunting of...

Doorman's Creek.

The scales of justice were met.

Rock of Realm by Lea Schizas

A lifelong sanctuary of home bliss suddenly comes to a halt when Alexandra Stone discovers her parents lied and kept secrets about their family heritage. The discovery comes after a silly chant transports Alex and her two pets, along with her best friend Sarah, to the outskirts of Rock Kingdom.

Now faced with the dangerous elements of Dread's Forest, Alex is determined to fight the man responsible for their predicament.

But is he responsible?

She will risk her safety and trust her instincts when thrust into battle with the Braks, skeletal creatures that project thorn-infested slime encasing their victim before plunging them deep within the caverns of the earth.

'Things are not always as they appear to be.' baffles Alex throughout her journey.

The Rock of Realm will shatter the concept of 'villain'.

Available in e-book and paperback.
EBOOK ISBN: 978-1-77392-084-9
PRINT ISBN: 978-1-77392-085-6

Stay in Touch

Join my newsletter for news on upcoming releases, exclusive content, free books, and more.

https://landing.mailerlite.com/webforms/landing/t8y2s0

ABOUT THE AUTHOR

Lea Schizas is a mother of five, grandmother, and wife to her high school sweetie. She's been "menditing" (mentoring and editing) authors and their books for over twenty-two years.

For up-to-date news on upcoming releases, contests, and just some fun, like and follow her on Facebook: https://www.facebook.com/LeaSchizasAuthorEditor

* * * *

Did you enjoy Doorman's Creek?
If so, please help spread the word.
It's as easy as:

•Recommend the book to your family and friends
•Post a review
•Tweet and Facebook about it

Thank you

www.ingramcontent.com/pod-product-compliance
Lightning Source LLC
LaVergne TN
LVHW091053150826
845673LV00002B/561

* 9 7 8 1 7 7 3 9 2 0 9 7 9 *